Bracebridge Hemyng, James H. Graff

Too Sharp by Half

Or, The Man Who Made Millions

Bracebridge Hemyng, James H. Graff

Too Sharp by Half
Or, The Man Who Made Millions

ISBN/EAN: 9783743399068

Manufactured in Europe, USA, Canada, Australia, Japa

Cover: Foto ©Andreas Hilbeck / pixelio.de

Manufactured and distributed by brebook publishing software (www.brebook.com)

Bracebridge Hemyng, James H. Graff

Too Sharp by Half

THE
SELECT LIBRARY OF FICTION.
PRICE *TWO SHILLINGS PER VOLUME.*

The best, cheapest, and most POPULAR NOVELS published, well printed
in clear, readable type, on good paper, and strongly bound.

Containing the writings of the most popular Authors of the day.

Of th   , there is none
which b   e hands of the
public th   lect Library of
Fiction.'   in themselves,
they pre   ed in clear and
excellent   y from some of
the chea   , and which so
sorely tr   ead in railway
carriages

n.

VOL.
1 Aga   ad, 672 pp., 3s.
                  Charles Lever.

2 Hea   *Charles Lever.*

                  pp., 3s.
5 The   *Charles Lever.*

                  772 pp., 3s.
7 Oliv   *Charles Lever.*

                  core
10 Mar   *Charles Lever.*

11 The   518 pp., 3s.
                  Charles Lever.

15 Rut   *Charles Lever.*

17 Jacl   sters
                  Emily Ponsonby.

18 Cha   Martin, 704 pp.,
                  Charles Lever.

20 The Daltons, 708 pp., 3s.
                  Charles Lever.

22 Harry Lorrequer's Confessions
                  Charles Lever.

23 Knight of Gwynne, 630 pp., 3s.
                  Charles Lever.

48 Sir Jasper Carew *Charles Lever.*

52 Young Heiress   *Mrs. Trollope.*

53 A Day's Ride; or, a Life's
   Romance   *Charles Lever.*

54 Maurice Tiernay *Charles Lever.*

THE SELECT LIBRARY OF FICTION.

VOL.

58 Master of the Hounds "*Scrutator.*"

60 Cardinal Pole : an Historical Novel   *W. H. Ainsworth.*

61 Jealous Wife   *Miss Pardoe.*

67 Charlie Thornhill *Charles Clarke.*

75 Barrington   *Charles Lever.*

77 Woman's Ransom   *F. W. Robinson.*

78 Deep Waters   *Anna H Drury.*

79 Misrepresentation   *Anna H. Drury.*

80 Tilbury Nogo   *Whyte Melville.*

82 He Would Be a Gentleman   *Samuel Lover.*

83 Mr. Stewart's Intentions   *F. W. Robinson.*

84 Mattie : a Stray   *Author of "Owen : a Waif."*

85 Doctor Thorne *Anthony Trollope.*

86 The Macdermots of Ballycloran   *Anthony Trollope.*

87 Lindisfarn Chase   *T. A. Trollope.*

88 Rachel Ray   *Anthony Trollope.*

89 Luttrell of Arran *Charles Lever.*

91 Wildflower   *F. W. Robinson.*

92 Irish Stories and Legends   *Samuel Lover.*

93 The Kellys and the O'Kellys   *Anthony Trollope.*

94 Married Beneath Him   *Author of " Found Dead."*

95 Tales of all Countries   *Anthony Trollope.*

96 Castle Richmond   *Anthony Trollope.*

99 Jack Brag   *Theodore Hook.*

VOL.

100 The Bertrams   *Anthony Trollope.*

101 Faces for Fortunes   *Augustus Mayhew.*

104 Under the Spell   *F. W. Robinson.*

105 Market Harborough   *Whyte Melville.*

106 Slaves of the Ring   *F. W. Robinson.*

111 One and Twenty   *F. W Robinson.*

112 Douglas's Vow   *Mrs. Edmund Jennings.*

113 Woodleigh   *F. W. Robinson.*

114 Theo Leigh   *Annie Thomas.*

116 Orley Farm, 589 pp., 3s.   *Anthony Trollope.*

117 Flying Scud   *Charles Clarke.*

118 Denis Donne   *Annie Thomas.*

119 Forlorn Hope   *Edmund Yates.*

120 Can you Forgive Her? 583 pp., 3s.   *Anthony Trollope.*

122 Miss Mackenzie   *Anthony Trollope.*

123 Carry's Confession   *By Author of " Mattie : a Stray."*

125 Belton Estate *Anthony Trollope.*

127 Dumbleton Common   *Hon. Eleanor Eden.*

128 Crumbs from a Sportsman's Table   *Charles Clarke.*

129 Bella Donna *Percy Fitzgerald.*

131 Christie's Faith   *By Author of "Mattie : a Stray."*

132 Polly : a Village Portrait   *By a Popular Writer.*

134 Called to Account   *Annie Thomas.*

THE SELECT LIBRARY OF FICTION.

VOL.

135 A Golden Heart
　　　　　　Tom Hood.

138 Clyffards of Clyffe
Author of " Married Beneath Him."

139 Which is the Winner
　　　　　　Charles Clarke.

140 Archie Lovell Mrs. Edwardes.

141 Lizzie Lorton E. Lynn Linton.

142 Milly's Hero F. W. Robinson.

143 Leo　　　　　Dutton Cook.

144 Uncle Silas　　J. S. Lefanu.

145 Bar Sinister Charles A. Collins.

146 Rose Douglas
　　　　　By a Popt

147 Cousin Stella ; or, (
　　　　　Mrs.

148 Highland Lassies
　　　　　Erick

149 Young Singleton
　　　　　Talb

150 The Eve of St. Mar
　　　　　Thomas

151 The Family Scapeg:
　　　　　J

152 Mirk Abbey
Author of " Married Ben

153 Fair Carew : or, Hu
　　　　　Wives

154 Riverston
　　　　　Georgiana M. Craik.

155 Sabina　　　Lady Wood.

156 Pique
　　　Author of "Agatha Beaufort."

157 Lord Falconberg's Heir
　　　　　Charles Clarke.

VOL.

158 A Fatal Error　J. Masterman.

159 Secret Dispatch James Grant,
　　　Author of " Romance of War."

160 Guy Deverell
　　　Author of " Uncle Silas."

161 Carr of Carrlyon Hamilton Aidé.

162 All in the Dark J. S. Lefanu.

163 Sense and Sensibility
　　　　　Jane Austen.

164 Emma　　　Jane Austen.

165 Mansfield Park　Jane Austen.

166 Northanger Abbey Jane Austen.

Prejudice
　　　　　Jane Austen.

or Father and Son
　　　　　Charles Clarke.

he Churchyard
　　　　　J. S. Lefanu.

Waif
" Mattie : a Stray."

ages
f " John Halifax."

d
rried Beneath Him."

or, How Mr. Blake
n M. F. H.
　　　　　Wat. Bradwood.

174 Foster Brothers　James Payn.

175 Robert-Houdin, Conjuror, &c.
　　　　　By Himself.

176 Only George
　　　Author of " Not Too Late."

177 Tenants of Malory
　　　　　J. S. Lefanu.

178 Wylder's Hand　J. S. Lefanu.

OTHER VOLUMES IN PREPARATION.

London : CHAPMAN & HALL, 193, Piccadilly.

TOO SHARP BY HALF;

OR,

THE MAN WHO MADE MILLIONS.

BY

BRACEBRIDGE HEMYNG,

AUTHOR OF "CURIOUS CRIMES," "THE FAVOURITE SCRATCHED," "SECRETS OF THE TURF," ETC., ETC.

LONDON:

CHARLES H. CLARKE, 13, PATERNOSTER ROW.

1871.

TOO SHARP BY HALF.

CHAPTER I.

MR. AND MRS. POMPUSS AND THEIR NIECE MYRA.

IT was a house on Highgate-hill. Not one of those
modern suburban erections, covered all over with stucco
and other meretricious adornments ; but a good solid
old-fashioned building. It had seen a few storms in its
time, and would, in all probability, have stood the
shock of an English earthquake without trembling. It
had a porch and a gate, and a few trees were scattered
here and there on the lawn. Not the cropped and
stunted limes that worry one's gaze in most places out
of London ; but an elm, an oak, and a cedar. The
cedar, with its black and sable foliage, was almost
grand in its antiquity. It was older than the house ;
it looked down upon the latter as of mushroom creation,
and it seemed to say, "I am of Lebanon, whilst you,
you were never dreamt of before the Georges came
over." This house belonged to Mr. John Pompuss, of
the firm of Pompuss and Co., Throgmorton-street, City,
Stockbrokers. Mr. Pompuss had bought it some years
ago, not because his taste was of a high order, but because it was cheap, and happened to be in the market
just when he was in want of some snug place to settle

B

down in. Mr. John Pompuss had done a good thing in Chicaraguan Bonds. He had obtained a little secret information—how never transpired—but acting upon this information, he had bought Chicaraguan at 9, and when a settlement of the debt took place he sold them again at 40. By this lucky hit Mr. Pompuss netted something like £15,000, which enabled him to remove from the neighbourhood of Charterhouse-square, where he had formerly been residing, to the more salubrious climate of Highgate. He had a wife, but he was child-less. His hearth, however, was enlivened by the pre-sence of his niece, Miss Myra Fontaine, a young lady a little more than eighteen years old, with a prospective fortune of £20,000. Her parents were both dead, and Mr. John Pompuss had undertaken the charge of his wife's brother's child when, at the age of sixteen, she had been left an orphan. Mr. Fontaine, in his will, gave his daughter his whole fortune, and made Mr. Pompuss sole executor.

An unsubstantial-looking French clock, probably an importation from the Rue de la Paix, had just in silvery tones struck the hour of nine, when a footfall was heard in the passage, a hand was laid upon the door-handle, and Mr. John Pompuss stood in the break-fast-room of his house on Highgate-hill. He glanced at the clock on the mantelpiece, took out his watch, compared the two, appeared satisfied with the com-parison, rang the bell for breakfast, and seating himself in an arm-chair, opened the *Times* newspaper, and was soon deeply immersed in its contents.

Hardly had the hissing urn made its appearance than Mrs. Pompuss came down stairs, and took her place at the head of the table. Her husband just glanced over the edge of his newspaper, and said, in the satisfied and authoritative tone which belonged to him—

"Make the tea, 'Liza."

Whilst this process was satisfactorily progressing, a knock, quickly followed by a ring, was heard at the door. A musical voice shortly afterwards called a dog, and Myra Fontaine walked into the breakfast-room.

Her face was very girlish and pretty—a little flushed with her morning walk, but glowing with a healthy colour ; long lashes fringed eyes of a deep blue ; her hair was light, very light, knotted behind and fastened with a comb. She despised that lazy contrivance, a net. It was not too much trouble for her to get up in the morning a quarter of an hour earlier, and do her hair. Her little mouth was red and rosy. Her nose was slightly inclined to turn up, but so slightly that it made her more interesting than if that important feature has been classic and regular. Her face was round and good-natured, but there was an indication of firmness and resolution about the corners of her mouth, which told you very plainly that she had a will of her own. She wore a velvet hat of a semi-conical shape, with a grebe feather along the side of it, for it was the beginning of autumn, and she had been renovating her wardrobe for their annual trip to Boulogne. Mr. and Mrs. John Pompuss always went to Boulogne. She had on a linsey dress, with the skirt scollopped at the edges. She thought that it was prettier and lighter for morning wear than velvet trimmings ; a jacket of a dark colour, made out of some frieze substance, surmounted her linsey dress, and the pockets outside were inviting for one's hands on a cold day. She had had this jacket made by a tailor. She was fond of saying that a milliner could make a dress, but could not possibly have any idea of making a jacket. She utterly abominated those wretched feminine absurdities called yachting jackets.

"I do not go yachting," she would say ; "and to wear anything supposed to resemble nautical costume is a sort of fraud upon the public ; besides, I should always be afraid that people would think it was 'This style, 17s. 6d.,' which you see in the shop-windows."

So she had her jacket modelled upon one of her uncle's, and made by his tailor, a worthy fellow in Fenchurch-street, who was thought a good deal of in the City.

Myra threw her hat upon the sofa, her jacket quickly followed her hat, and she took her place at the breakfast-table in an elegant little waistcoat, made to match her dress, and constructed of the same material. Her collar and cuffs matched one another; the former was fastened with a gold stud, and the cuffs with sleeve-links of rather a masculine pattern, which were very pretty and becoming. The cuffs and collar were striped with black.

Mr. Pompuss laid down his newspaper at a summons from his wife, and prepared for breakfast. He was stout and thick-set, rather under the average height; his hair was beginning to fall off a little about the temples, as it does occasionally with men who are on the shady side of forty.

Mrs. Pompuss was thin and delicate, with tiny regular features, quite doll-like. She was now five and thirty, and still fragile and *mignonne*. The only change which had taken place in her since Mr. Pompuss led her to the altar, fifteen years ago, was that her hair was darker, and, if it must be confessed, a little thinner at the parting, and a gentle, almost sad, expression sat at times upon her marionette countenance. Myra ascribed this to the effect of her religious tendencies; for her aunt sat under Dr. Cumming, and was eternally dreading some great convulsion of nature, some cataclysm, some convincing evidence of irresistible celestial wrath; and the burden of her song at matins and vespers was, "Teach me to live, that I may die." All this was very estimable in its way, but, as Mr. John Pompuss was accustomed to say—

"Religion is all very well, Sir; but it's possible to have too much of a good thing."

"Deluded man!" his wife would reply, solemnly; "you serve Mammon."

" I don't know about Mammon," Mr. Pompuss would mutter to himself; "but I should like to know where the bread and cheese would come from if I did not look after it. Mammon! Yes, it's all very fine. But the bread and cheese, Sir—the bread and cheese!"

" Had a nice walk, my dear?" said Mr. Pompuss, carving a chicken.

" Capital, uncle! I have been to the top of the hill and back again," replied Myra.

" Nothing like it," said Mr. Pompuss; "nothing like it. Stick to that, and you'll live till you're seventy."

" Seventy, uncle! You ought to be ashamed of yourself; as if ladies ever did live so long. Don't you know that they are like fairies; their age is always a matter of conjecture and uncertainty—generally below thirty, but never exceeding thirty-five."

" Ah! you are on the right side of the post," replied Mr. Pompuss, " and you can afford to laugh; but I don't know what I should do if I had no exercise. Why, I believe I should get stout."

Although Mr. Pompuss was undoubtedly so already, he would never concede the fact. It was one of his peculiarities.

" I admit," he continued, as he perceived a smile on his niece's lips, " that I am a decent size for an Englishman; but not stout—by no means stout."

" What exercise can you have, uncle, being in the City, as you are, all day long?"

" That, my dear, is the very place where I do take exercise. My offices, you know, or ought to know, are a little way from Capel-court, and I have sometimes to go into the 'house' a hundred times a-day. As matters on the Stock Exchange admit of no delay, I am obliged to hurry to and fro; and I can tell you that I am as tired sometimes, when I come home, as if I had walked to Hampstead Heath and back, without having a glass of ale at Jack Straw's Castle."

"You seem in good spirits to-day, John," exclaimed Mrs. Pompuss.

"Couldn't be better, my dear—couldn't be better!" answered her husband, who was fond of repeating his sentences.

"Are you a Bull or a Bear—eh, uncle? I believe those are the proper terms, are they not?" said Myra.

"A little of both," replied Mr. Pompuss. I am Bearing Metropolitan and Bulling Greek, and I think I shall have a go-in at Mexican to-day, if the jobbers will do an operation on reasonable terms. A man in my office lost a cool thousand yesterday through that drop in Venezuelan. But I see my friend S——, of the City Article, gives the stock a lift this morning; so I shouldn't wonder if prices are better to-day."

"How fond you are of talking shop, uncle," said Myra, mischievously.

"Shop! Well, what's the odds? Every man to his own trade. But you are just like your father. He was always fastidious in his tastes. His name was Thomas Lovaine—wasn't it, Lizzie? And he dropped the Tom and called himself Lovaine Fontaine. I am only a stockbroker; I know that. But I could show you a dozen stockbrokers and jobbers who could buy up half the Peerage as easily as I can say Jack Robinson. Not that I object to the aristocracy, individually; but, in the abstract, I think they're a stuck-up lot. Now, I shouldn't mind you making a good marriage; and you would be a catch for a man with a title without any money, and your face and your money's as good as an earldom any day."

At this allusion to matrimony Myra's face changed colour. Mrs. Pompuss looked at her husband deprecatingly, as if she did not wish him to carry on the subject any further. But of all blundering animals there is none that goes so thoroughly into the mud as your well-intentioned Englishman.

" Now, there's that man on the direction of the Great Eastern Hotel Company—the one I'm broker for ; you know who I mean, Lizzy—Sir Philip Deverill. He's got no money, and I believe the two guineas a-week he pockets for coming to the board meetings helps him over the stile a bit. But then he is a baronet, you know."

" Only a baronet, uncle !" exclaimed Myra, slyly glancing at her aunt.

" Well, he's only a baronet ; I know that. Of course, Sir John Bullock, of Bullock and Robarts', would be a very nice fish for anybody's net; but there are some fish which won't bite, and beggars must not be choosers."

" Why, uncle, one would think you had been writing copies for a Sunday-school," cried Myra, laughing.

" Well, you can laugh," replied Mr. Pompuss, "but you may go farther and do worse than Sir Philip, I can tell you."

" Are you joking, or are you in earnest, dear uncle ?" exclaimed Myra, looking up in his face anxiously.

" Never more in earnest in my life," answered her uncle. " You're getting on, you know, Myra ; and you are old enough to think of these things, and Lady Deverill wouldn't sound badly, in my opinion ; and when you went to Court you would hold up your head as proudly as any of them."

Myra looked annoyed for a second, and then she exclaimed, as her face brightened a little—

" ' Lady Deverill, by the Duchess of Capel-court, on her marriage," wouldn't sound badly. But that is a new idea of yours, uncle. Why don't you go to Court ? ' Mr. John Pompuss, on having made a good spec. in Metropolitans, by Lord Sixteen-five-eighths-seven-eighths.' How would that read ?"

"You're as impudent as you're pretty," replied Mr. Pompuss. "But I am in a good humour this morning; so I sha'n't scold you. But you think over what I have told you. Sir Philip has noticed you when he has dined here, and he put some questions to me the other day which showed me which way the wind blows."

"Oh! Sir Philip has noticed me," said Myra, elevating her eyebrows. "So you really mean that, uncle? Did the baronet actually condescend to notice poor me?"

"Yes, Myra; there's no doubt of it—no doubt whatever. He's a little sweet in a certain quarter, or else I shouldn't say so," replied Mr. John Pompuss, happily innocent of the sarcasm intended to be conveyed in his niece's speech.

As will be seen, Mr. Pompuss, like a great many others, was a contradiction. He affected to despise rank, and thought only of the aristocracy of wealth; but although this was his openly-avowed creed, he did not conceal his partiality for a title, considered *per se* and not taken as an aggregate of the British Peerage.

"Now I must be off," he suddenly exclaimed, rising from his chair, and buttoning his coat.

Myra rang the bell, and the servant brought his master's hat and umbrella. (Mr. Pompuss never moved out of the house without the latter appendage.) Mr. Pompuss consulted his watch—a splendid chronometer, for which he had given Benson ninety guineas—and said—

"Ten o'clock! Run to the gate, William, and stop the 'bus. If I miss it, I sha'n't get to the City in time for business; and I wouldn't be away when the market opens, for untold gold."

The servant ran to obey his master's orders, just succeeded in catching the omnibus, and in another minute Mr. John Pompuss, who was his own Co., was rumbling along towards his office.

The two ladies were left together.

CHAPTER II.

"THE ODDS ARE TWO TO ONE."

AFTER Mr. Pompuss had left for the City, Myra remained in a state of abstraction. Mrs. Pompuss—or 'Liza, as her liege lord was fond of calling her—sat still, reading the paper, and occasionally sipping her tea. She was looking for those wars and rumours of wars, those sudden deaths and bloody murders, those accidents by flood and field, which were continually dinned into her ears by the Prophet of Crown-court. Fortunately for his predictions, the world is so bad and evilly-disposed that a day seldom passes without an announcement of something of the kind. On the present occasion Mrs. Pompuss was extremely gratified by reading an account of the murder of a husband by being thrown down a well, and of a subsequent bigamy by the murderess; but her disgust was great and unfathomable when she discovered that she had just taken the review of a fashionable novel for an actual occurrence.

Myra was aroused from her reverie by her pet dog, a silky-haired sky. The little creature pawed its mistress's dress and whined; it had had no breakfast.

"Poor Toy!" said Myra. "Hasn't it been fed ? What a naughty Missie, not to feed her poor dogs! Come along, my petsy one."

The "petsy one" wagged its tail at railroad speed, and the "naughty Missie" gave it a plateful of bones, and bread and butter, saying, as she did so—

"There, Toy, you won't hurt if you eat all that."

When Toy had finished his breakfast, he again came forward, wagging his everlasting tail ; but Myra did not greet his advances so favourably.

"Go away," she cried, impatiently.

But as Toy persisted in his attentions, she caught him by the neck and pinched his ears in a manner not exactly indicative of love and kindness.

After the disappointment in the "well case," Mrs. Pompuss laid the paper down, and looked across the table at her niece.

"A penny for your thoughts, Myra!" she exclaimed, playfully.

"They're not worth it. You shall have them for nothing," replied Myra. "I was thinking about what uncle was saying at breakfast-time."

"You mean about Sir Philip Deverill?"

"Yes, I do, aunt dear. Was my uncle really in earnest about my marrying him?" said Myra.

"In earnest, child? Of course. You know he never jokes about a thing of that kind. I am sure Sir Philip is a very nice gentleman, and would make an agreeable addition to our small family."

"You and uncle seem to have made up your minds on the matter," replied Myra, looking very much annoyed.

"We have talked the matter over, my dear Myra, certainly we have," said Mrs. Pompuss; "and, as we have your good at heart, we could be actuated by no unworthy feeling. We think that it is the best thing that you can do. I had promised John that I would talk to you about it; but, in his blundering way, he said all he had to say this morning. Really, men have no tact, and his thoughts, poor man, are always, always fixed upon Mammon."

"Oh, never mind Mammon, aunt !" said Myra, stamping her little foot on the floor.

Mrs. Pompuss looked up in considerable surprise. She was not altogether unaccustomed to these exhibitions of temper on the part of her niece ; but she did not expect one of them on the present occasion.

"You must not be so hasty, my dear Myra. If you do not learn to control your temper, Heaven only knows what will become of you," said Mrs. Pompuss.

"Suppose I do not like this man—this Sir Philip Deverill?" she exclaimed, not heeding her aunt's remark.

"You surely would not be so blind to your own interest?"

"Excuse me, dear aunt, but I know my own interest quite as well, if not better, than you do," replied Myra.

"Well, Miss Fontaine," said her aunt, rather sternly, "let us hear what your idea of your own interest is."

"Not to marry Sir Philip Deverill," answered Myra, firmly.

"Oh, nonsense, child ; you don't know your own mind."

"First I don't know my own interest, and then I don't know my own mind! Don't, please don't, treat me like a child, aunt," exclaimed Myra, passionately

"You never will be so foolish as to reject a man who really loves you, who will give you a position in the world, and ——"

"I will," broke in Myra, shortly.

"Then you will not be so wicked as to fly in the face of your uncle and myself, and to do the exact opposite of what we wish you?"

"Oh! what shall I do?" said Myra, burying her face in her hands, and sobbing violently.

Mrs. Pompuss rose, and, walking towards her niece, stroked her hair, and said, "Think of what I have said, my dear child, and pray for counsel and guidance ; and when we meet at lunch you will, I daresay, be in a better and more obedient frame of mind than you are at present."

A minute or so Myra continued to sob as if her heart would break ; but her temperament was so volatile that this could not continue long. The hardest rain is the soonest over ; so it is with tears. Lifting up her head, she said aloud—

"I won't marry him. They may be both against me ; but I wont, I won't, I won't ! "

Her spirit asserted its independence, and the battle began. But the odds were two to one.

13

CHAPTER III.

THE GRAND TRUNK OF BOHEMIA.

THE reason why Mr. John Pompuss was so elated at
breakfast-time was not because he was a Bull of Greek
or a Bear of Metropolitans, or because he wished to do an
operation on anything like reasonable terms in Mexican,
but because a speculation in which he was deeply
interested had come out at a very good premium, and
had been favourably mentioned in the *Times*. Mr.
Pompuss had been bitten with the mania that people
sometimes indulge in of becoming suddenly rich. Fatal
mistake! Ruinous error! The Grand Trunk Railway
of Bohemia was an undertaking which, according to the
prospectus, must pay between forty and fifty per cent. on
the paid-up capital. One of his richest clients had gone
into Grand Trunks on a large scale, and when Mr. Pompuss arrived, he found several people with smiling faces
awaiting his arrival. He first nodded to each, spoke a
word or two to his clerks, and then hurried through
Bartholomew-lane to the market. His return was
awaited with impatience.

"Well, Pompuss," exclaimed Mr. Isaac Moskins, the
rich client before alluded to, "how are Grand Trunks?"

"Grand Trunks, a little flat; seven-eighths, one and
an eighth—Mexican, twenty-six, flat; Greek, twenty-four
and a-half, three-quarters—decidedly good; Metropolitan,
flat, same as yesterday; Universal Banks, three-eighths
premium; Submarine Railroads, four dis.; Great Eastern,
nowhere, can't get a price for it; Hammersmith Hotels,
a quarter premium; Giant Balloon, par to a half, three-

quarters ; Consols, quarter to a half for money, account five-eighths, seven-eighths."

"Grand Trunks flat, are they?" said Mr. Moskins. "What is the cause of it?"

"Oh, realizing," replied Mr. Pompuss. "The fact is, these things come out at a premium, and then a lot of fellows go and sell Bears of them, and that keeps the market down."

"What would you do under the circumstances?"

"Under the circumstances, I should buy."

"You would?"

"Most decidedly. I think you'll have 'em ten premium—I do, indeed," replied Mr. Pompuss.

"You hold a good many, I think you said," exclaimed Mr. Moskins.

Mr. Pompuss approached, and putting his hand up to his mouth, went close to his client and whispered something in his ear.

"God bless me!" cried Mr. Moskins. "Well, you ought to know."

"You see Bohemia is a country capable of great development."

"So it is."

"And a railroad opens up the resources of a country; for where would England be without her railroads?"

"That's true!"

"Very well, then," continued Mr. Pompuss, "what will the future of Bohemia be? Why, splendid, Sir—splendid. The traffic will be enormous, and the produce of the country will come over here in thousands of tons, Sir—thousands of tons; I have no hesitation in saying, in thousands of tons."

"You think now is a good time to buy?"

"To be sure. Buy them, and lock them up. A thousand or two won't hurt you—eh, Moskins? There's more where that will come from."

Mr. Pompuss said this jocularly, giving his rich client a dig in the ribs.

"Well, Pompuss, I'll tell you what I'll do. Another thousand! That'll make three I've got; and then I'll drop it. I shall lock 'em up at the banker's, and there they may stop."

"That's just my way when I get hold of a good thing," replied Pompuss. "Why, look at Chicaraguan. I bought it at 9, and locked it up, and—well, never mind. I didn't lose anything by it. Shall I buy you a thousand?"

"If you please," said Mr. Moskins; "and bring the stock out of the market with you."

"I say, Pompuss!" cried Mr. Moskins, as the broker was leaving the office.

Mr. Pompuss turned round and came back to his client, who said—

"By the way, I don't exactly like the look of political affairs."

"They are a little shaky."

"What about Consols?"

"Well, there are good buyers."

"But the French Funds became worse yesterday."

"I know; there is nothing in that, though," replied Mr. Pompuss. "The fall was only ten centimes."

"I should like to Bear Consols. To tell you the truth, I don't like the aspect of affairs in Prussia. I think I should like you to sell fifty thousand."

"Fifty thousand! Very well. I'm going into the market, and I'll do it for you."

Mr. Pompuss left the office, and went into the house. He was absent about a quarter of an hour. While he was gone Mr. Moskins read the *Morning Post*.

Mr. Moskins was a tea dealer and grocer at the West-end. He was known to be very rich, and he now and then turned a penny on the Stock Exchange. He was a very good client of Mr. Pompuss, and that gentleman was not a bit afraid to act for him, even to a large extent. The banks would do Mr. Isaac Moskins' bill for ten thousand for a month, at two and a-half or three per cent., any day, except when the Money Market was unusually tight, when they would probably charge a little more. He was a coarse, common-looking man, and had the least possible tinge of Jewish extraction about him. This had been toned down through successive generations and inter-marriage with the Gentile, but the trace remained. There was still a tang of the cask in him, as it were.

When Mr. Pompuss returned, he said, " I've done that for you, Moskins. I've got the Trunks at seven-eighths, and sold the Consols at a half."

Mr. Moskins expressed himself satisfied with this arrangement, and took his leave, saying he should come back in the afternoon to see how the market closed. Things were good, and Mr. Moskins smilingly shook hands with his broker. But in the middle of the day a cloud came over the market. Mr. Reuter's agents telegraphed bad news from Bohemia. It appeared that the price of land had risen, and there was some opposition to the granting of the compulsory charter, which had been regarded as a *fait accompli*. Grand Trunks relapsed, and went down to six discount. Mr. Pompuss was quite astounded, and endeavoured to sell some of the stock he held, but the only price he could get for it was so preposterously low that he thought it better to hold it, as there would most likely be a reaction after so great a fall. At half-past three things were worse. Bohemian Grand Trunks were as low as eight and a-half. This was the state of things when Mr. Moskins drove up in a Hansom to the office in Throgmorton-street, and sought Mr. Pompuss. That gentleman had just returned from the market, and was looking very pale and harassed.

" How are Consols now ? I needn't ask you about Grand Trunks, for they are sure to be better," said Mr. Moskins.

" Consols, quarter to a half; Trunks, eight to nine discount," replied Mr. Pompuss, almost mechanically He seemed like a parrot repeating a set phrase.

" Premium, you mean," said Mr. Moskins. " Come now, you needn't joke with me, Pompuss."

Mr. Pompuss made no answer.

" Well, what is the cause of the rise ?" continued Mr. Moskins. " Rather sudden, wasn't it ?"

Mr. Pompuss turned round slowly, and said to one of his clerks, " Delmar, what are Grand Trunks ?"

" Eight to nine dis., Sir," replied the clerk quickly, instantly busying himself in his accounts again.

" By Jingo !" cried Mr. Moskins, biting his right-hand thumb-nail. " What are we to do ?"

" I don't know ; 'pon my word, I don't," replied Mr. Pompuss.

" Stand and be shot at—eh ?"

" We must stand the racket, I suppose, and wait till things get better. Who could have expected this ?" answered Mr. Pompuss. " Hardy Brothers were buying up Trunks like steam this morning. Oh, they'll get better. It is a fall—there is no doubt about that ; but they must go up again before long."

" Do you think it's a rig ?" asked Mr. Moskins.

" Shouldn't wonder if it was," replied the broker. " You see, there was a telegram about the price of land having risen in Bohemia, and the Bohemian Government make some difficulty about parting with the land as they agreed to do. But it looks confoundedly like a cock and a bull story, or like what the French call a ' duck.' The devil of it is, though, that the stock has gone down. They are all sellers ; in fact, there's no

c

market. It's like Confederate Loan after the Battle of Gettysburg."

Mr. Moskins thought a moment, and then said—

"Pompuss, go in and buy me ten thousand Grand Trunks."

"Excuse me, but ——" began Mr. Pompuss.

"What?"

"Only this; suppose the stock goes down?"

"Well, I can afford to pay the money, I suppose," replied Mr. Moskins.

"Oh, no doubt; but—eh? The fact is, I should like a little more cover."

Mr. Moskins looked a moment at the stammering broker, and then took his cheque-book out of his pocket. Seizing a pen, he hastily wrote a draft for five thousand pounds.

"Will that do for you?" he said.

"Perfectly satisfied, my dear Sir. Don't want to offend you, you know—don't want to offend anybody; but business is business, and I must protect myself."

With these words, Mr. Pompuss went into the market, having just taken the precaution to give the cheque to one of his clerks, telling him to pay it in before four. When the jobbers saw that Pompuss, who was well known as a prudent man, was buying, they raised the price, and shortly before four Grand Trunks were quoted four to five discount. When Mr. Moskins heard this he went to another broker of his, and told him to sell five thousand Trunks. When this was accomplished he went to another, and sold ten thousand. This showed the versatility of his genius, and Grand Trunks were finally marked seven discount.

At the close of business, Mr. Pompuss struck his forehead with his hand, and muttered to himself—

"What the devil shall I do? I never was in such a scrape in my life before. Grand Trunks at seven, and

I hold five and twenty thousand. I must get out of it somehow. Let me see. Deverill? No; he's no good. Moskins? Ah! Moskins."

He cogitated a moment, and at last exclaimed aloud—

"If Moskins is properly worked, he will get me out of the mud."

CHAPTER IV

Mr. Moskins is Properly Worked.

During the few days that had to elapse before the Saturday half-holiday closed the week, the position of Grand Trunks of Bohemia was anything but encouraging. They fluctuated widely between seven and ten discount, and on Saturday they closed at the latter figure. Mr. John Pompuss was visibly annoyed at so unfavourable a state of things; but he endeavoured to keep up the spirits of his client, Mr. Moskins, by repeatedly assuring him that there would be a rally before long. It was a little remarkable that Mr. Pompuss was unusually civil to his rich client, and on the Saturday in question he begged him to come back to Highgate and have what he was pleased to call "a bit of dinner."

"I really can't say what my wife has for us," he remarked, "but you must come and take pot-luck with us. We are fellow-sufferers in this Bohemian undertaking, and we ought to be better acquainted. What do you say?"

Mr. Moskins doubted his ability to come on that particular Saturday.

"Now, don't say no; I won't have a refusal. I am one of those men who won't take 'No' for an answer when they set their hearts on anything," replied Mr. Pompuss.

Mr. Moskins still hesitated.

"Ah! I see, the fact is that you don't like the idea of pot-luck. You're a knowing fellow, Moskins," said Mr. Pompuss, pleasantly. "Well, I'll tell you what we'll do. We'll run down to the Ship at Greenwich, and have a snack there, and come up to my place and tap a bottle of my twenty-four Madeira; or I can give you a glass of port you don't meet with every day. Sandyman's vintage, Sir, 1818—Sandyman's vintage. 'Pon my word, Carbonnel has'nt anything like it—offered me ten guineas a-dozen for all I had left."

"Well, I don't mind if I do run out of town for an hour with you," replied Mr. Moskins. "I am rather annoyed at this continued declension in Grand Trunks, and perhaps a run into the country will do me good."

"Done, Sir," cried Mr. Pompuss, in great glee; "give us your hand on it, old boy."

"How will you go—rail, river, or cab?"

"Oh! get into a boat, I think."

"All right; I'm your man. Just excuse me for a moment; I have a letter or two to write. I won't keep you a minute."

"You write your letters; never mind me. I am going on to Garraway's. Perhaps you will come after me—eh?"

"With pleasure, Sir, with pleasure; join you at Garraway's in a quarter of an hour."

Mr. Moskins left the office, and Mr. Pompuss sat down and wrote the following letter:—

"Dear 'Liza,—Heard me talk of Moskins, haven't you? Tea dealer, grocer, and in dry goods, and all that, West-end; got no end of money—buy up the Bank of England almost. Going to dine with me at Greenwich. Back to dessert and coffee about nine o'clock. Get up a bottle or two of that Madeira I bought at Wyld's sale, the other day; and tell Myra to get herself up, you know, something out of the common. *I want her to make an impression.* Moskins isn't to be sneezed at; worth a dozen Sir Philip Deverills. Isn't fit to tie Moskins' shoe-strings. Expect me at nine, not later ; and don't forget about Myra.—Yours, in haste,

" JOHN POMPUSS."

After dispatching this to his house at Highgate, Mr. Pompuss paid in, locked up his safe, took up his hat and gloves, and walked over to Garraway's. As he was going through the Royal Exchange, he ran up against Sir Philip Deverill.

" Ah ! how are you ? Quite well ? Glad to hear it," exclaimed Mr. Pompuss.

" It's all up with Grand Trunks," said Sir Philip, hastily, as if he was possessed of some news that it was incumbent upon him to get rid of immediately.

" How do you know ?" asked Mr. Pompuss.

" Never you mind, my dear fellow. You take my advice, and get rid of them," replied Sir Philip, oracularly.

" I know they are at a discount ; but what of that ? They'll rally, Sir—they'll rally."

" You think so ; and so do some other fellows I know But I have just heard something which will make Grand Trunks open nowhere on Monday morning."

" What—what do you mean ?" gasped Mr. Pompuss, bursting into a cold sweat all over.

" Only this. Now, you won't let it go any further ?"

" No, no," replied the broker, in an agony of impatience.

" You give me your word of that, Pompuss ?"

" Yes, yes. For God's sake, go a-head."

" So I will. Don't be in a hurry. You are the sort of man who can afford a loss, Pompuss, I hope ; or else ——"

" Else what ?"

" Well, a nod's as good as a wink," said Sir Philip Deverill, trying to look very wise.

" Will you speak ?" said the broker, in despairing accents. "What the devil is this infernal news which is to send the stock down to zero—eh ?"

" Well, I'll tell you. War was declared at ten o'clock this morning between Bohemia and Montenegro."

"God bless my soul !" cried Mr. Pompuss; " you don't say so."

" Fact, I assure you. Had it just now from the chairman of Great Saharas—particular friend of mine ; and he ought to know."

" Are the Moteniggers ——"

" Negrins," suggested Sir Philip.

" Are they warlike ? Have they got a standing army ?" asked Mr. Pompuss.

" Splendid standing army, organized Militia, and subsidized by the Porte," replied Sir Philip Deverill. " Sure to smash Bohemia altogether. And then what becomes of your Trunks—eh, my dear Pompuss ?"

Mr. Pompuss tried to look cheerful as he said, " Doesn't matter to me, Sir Philip. Glad to say I sold mine this morning. Slight loss, of course; but as I didn't like the look of them, I thought it was better to get rid of them right off; so I washed my hands of them."

Sir Philip looked at him incredulously, but replied, "I congratulate you. Glad to hear it, my dear Pompuss. By the way, how is that charming niece of yours ? Flatter myself I made an impression in that quarter —eh, Pompuss ?"

Mr. Pompuss replied that Myra was not in very good health, and had gone into the country to visit some friends for a few days.

" I'm sorry for that," remarked Sir Philip ; " made up my mind to call upon you, and feel my way a bit this evening."

" Delighted to see you, I am sure, Sir Philip, at any

time ; as, of course, I need not tell you ; but to-night I sha'n't be at home, unfortunately, as I am going to dine at Greenwich," replied Mr. Pompuss.

Sir Philip Deverill looked rather disappointed at this unexpected news.

"Tell you what, Sir Philip.   Look in some day next week ; will you say Thursday ?   She'll be at home then, and you can do the amiable."

Sir Philip promised compliance, and they parted.

Mr. Moskins was at Garraway's, standing at the bar and eating a sandwich.

" You'll spoil your appetite," said Mr. Pompuss.

" Not at all," replied Mr. Moskins, " not at all, Sir. A sandwich and a glass of sherry is a whet !"

Mr. Pompuss indulged in a glass of sherry, and then, linking his arm in that of his friend, walked down to the Old Swan Pier, to catch the Greenwich boat.

CHAPTER V

BUYING A WIFE.

THE attractions of Greenwich are for Cœlebs, and such
as he ; Benedict knows them not. Such is the opinion
of a confiding wife. Mr. Isaac Moskins, however, was
not troubled with the encumbrance of a wife, although
he made no secret of his desire to meet with someone
whom he could make his own. He was sufficiently
romantic to declare that he expected, and absolutely
required, the poetic accompaniments of a milk-white
skin, hair like virgin gold, and other attributes that one
thinks of in a Tennysonian dream of fair women. But
Mr. Isaac Moskins was going on for fifty, and he was
very silly to indulge in such fancies. The only explana-
tion of such an absurdity is that men on the shady side
of forty are generally exacting. The rich grocer and
tea dealer's chance of realizing his dream consisted in
his wealth ; for as long as there are wealthy men to woo,
there will be lovely women to wed. If beautiful girls
object to sell themselves for gold, avaricious mothers
will drive the bargain for them. Sometimes, not unfre-
quently, the prettiest girls are the poorest, and they
will sacrifice themselves in order to smooth the declining
years of aged parents, and allow them to go down to the
grave in peace. Mr. Moskins had been some years
seeking for his paragon, and he had not found it yet ; but
he did not despair. He argued, " I have money, and I
can offer a woman jewels and dresses, and opera-boxes,
and houses, and carriages, and horses, and " —his baits

were numerous—"in addition to this, I can offer her love."

What Mr. Moskins' love was worth, is a question for those who have studied the development of the amorous passion in men of mature years. For my part, I do not believe in it.

Mr. Pompuss was well aware that his friend was in search of a wife, and he had marked him for his own. Sir Philip Deverill was placed upon the shelf until the way in which the wind blew was decided by the Pompussian weathercock. If human means could compass it, Myra should be Mrs. Moskins. With this end in view, the stockbroker was very civil, and made himself excessively agreeable to his West-end millionaire.

The table at which the two men were seated was close to a window, which was half open, allowing the air of the river, such as it was, to float into the room. On the present occasion it was not so bad as it is popularly supposed to be, as the tide had been flowing in for some time, and was nearly flood. Consequently the perennial mud-larks were absent from their native soil, and poor Jack was probably engaged in a by no means unnecessary ablution.

The craft on the river was moving swiftly up towards the docks. The Ostend boat, which had just left St. Katharine's-wharf, was steaming gaily down, unconscious of "*mal de mer*" off the Foreland, and happily ignorant of the predictions of Admiral Fitzroy, the diviner of the secrets of the Cave of Æolus.

White-bait had been consumed in at least twenty different shapes. The waiter had uncorked the fifth bottle of Moselle, and as his heart warmed towards all mankind, Mr. Moskins wiped his mouth with his napkin, placed it on his knees, which were studiously crossed, and looking at his friend, exclaimed—

"I'll tell you what it is, Pompuss."

Mr. Pompuss looked up at this announcement with just the least tinge of curiosity upon his countenance.

"In my opinion," continued Mr. Moskins, "there are worse places to dine at than Greenwich."

Issue not being joined, the resolution was carried unanimously. The stockbroker did not contradict his friend in any instance; he carefully avoided giving him any offence, and he did not think it worth while to tell him the important news about Grand Trunks which he had learned from Sir Philip Deverill as he was leaving the City. He had his own reasons for wishing Mr. Moskins to be in the best possible humour; and when the shades of evening began to draw closer together, the two men returned to town, and, getting into a cab, drove to Highgate. Here Mrs. Pompuss received her husband's guest with great urbanity, and he was ushered into the drawing-room which had been prepared for his reception.

Myra was seated upon a lounge, abstractedly playing with a Chinese puzzle. She looked very charming, although she could not have been more plainly dressed. She wore a white muslin dress, with a blue sash tied round her waist. A string of pearls circled her neck, and on her wrist glittered a small gold bracelet, upon which was engraved, in Gothic characters, "*Je vous aime.*" This was a present from Frank Ogilvie, the curate of the parish; and it seldom left her arm. She wore no rings.

Myra looked up as her uncle entered the room, followed by his guest, and laid the puzzle down upon her lap.

Mr. Moskins' bow was returned rather frigidly; but nothing disconcerted, he sat himself down by her side, and commenced a conversation which his fair companion did all she could to show him possessed no interest for her. At last, the servant brought in the coffee, and Mr.

Moskins got up and joined his host, who was standing near the fireplace.

Mr. Pompuss had been watching all this with ill-disguised dissatisfaction. He was much annoyed that Myra did not care to make herself more agreeable; so, by way of a diversion, he exclaimed, "Give me a little music, will you, Myra?"

Myra made no answer, but walked across the room to the piano. Seating herself, she played a selection from *Trovatore*, muttering to herself, "I suppose that is the sort of thing he likes. All City men like *Traviata* and *Trovatore*. The *Barbière* and the *Prophète* are a little beyond them."

The piano was one of Erard's, and Myra did it justice. Her execution was brilliant and faultless.

Mr. Moskins was delighted; he turned to Pompuss, and said, "By Jove, Sir! Arabella Goddard couldn't beat that; not she. I'd back your niece against her any day in the week."

Mr. Pompuss smiled, and said, " 'Sh-sh!" as if he were so pleased he did not wish to lose a note of the music. But the dealer in dry goods was not to be suppressed; he went on in spite of his friend's admonition.

"She's a way of her own, though. Now, you'd hardly believe it, but I tried all I knew to draw her out; but, hang me! if she'd leave her shell; no, Sir, she wouldn't."

With a dash and a clatter, Myra brought her selection to a close. Without paying any attention to the kind thanks of Mr. Moskins, she got up and sat down by the side of her aunt, who said, "Very nicely played, my dear; but a little too noisy, just a leetle."

"Oh, snobs like noise," replied Myra, taking up a book, and restlessly turning over the pages.

Mr. Pompuss saw the evident interest his rich visitor took in Myra, and he thought that it would be more prudent to take him away for a little while, as his niece was evidently in no amiable mood. So he suggested that "an anchovy toast and a glass of that choice Madeira wouldn't be amiss."

Mr. Moskins made no objection, and, arm-in-arm, they walked across the passage to the dining-room.

"A splendid creature, Sir!" exclaimed Mr. Moskins, as the two men sat down over their wine. "A really fine thing in women, Sir!"

The stockbroker smiled, and replied that "It wasn't the first time he had been told so."

"Now, that is my sort of girl," continued Mr. Moskins. "How old is she?"

"About nineteen."

"Rising nineteen. Capital age, Sir! Do anything with a woman if you get her young enough; mould her and shape her, and form her into anything, like a bit of dough, Sir, or a lump of clay."

"She's got some money, too," said Mr. Pompuss.

"Ah!"

"Yes, a matter of twenty thousand, when she comes of age."

"Now, look here, Pompuss," suddenly exclaimed Mr. Moskins.

The stockbroker drew his chair closer.

"I'm a man of few words. I don't talk much, like your sheep's heads of fellows—eh?"

"Certainly not."

"Very well, then. Now, look you here. I'm going to be a little short; but it's my way, as you know."

Mr. Pompuss replied that he had that honour and satisfaction, and helped his friend to a third glass of that choice Madeira.

"Now, you look here, Pompuss. I'll tell you what it is. I'm a man of few words, as you know; but I mean what I say, and I say what I mean, which is more than most men do; and this is what I'm going to say to you."

Mr. Pompuss looked as if he could not, for the life of him, guess what his friend was going to say.

"I'll marry that girl, Pompuss," said Mr. Moskins, abruptly. There was a pause, when he added, " I'm rich, richer than some people think. Why, Sir, twenty thousand's a flea-bite to me. And rich men can afford to do eccentric things. Why, Sir, the power of money's incalculable. You should see the girls and mothers almost crawling on the ground to me. But I see through them, Sir; and that sort of thing doesn't wash. I saw *your* game, Pompuss, directly, you old Slyboots; and I thought I'd play with you as I've played with many another before; but, hang me! if I haven't fallen into my own trap. I like that girl's independent spirit, and I think I have found Miss Right at last. By the way, Pompuss, there's no previous attachment, is there? No stuff of that sort; no poor curate, briefless barrister, or penniless younger son; is there?"

"None at all, my dear Sir; none at all," Mr. Pompuss hastened to assure him.

"I have your word for that?"

"Certainly you have."

"All right, all right; only I like to be on the right side of the hedge, that's all," replied Mr. Moskins.

"Quite so."

"No offence, I hope; none meant."

"None at all. Quite natural. But ——"

"Eh?" ejaculated Mr. Moskins.

"You see, it will be a delicate matter to manage; and a good deal rests with me, as the guardian, of course. If she attempted to marry without my consent, Sir, I should make her a ward in Chancery, with the least possible delay."

" Ah !" said Mr. Moskins, with a smile, " I said you were a Slyboots, Pompuss. I know a fox when I see him ; rather reckon I do, too. Fact is, you want to feather your nest, Pompuss ; and only natural, too. I see no objection to such a proceeding. Now, don't, don't say ' No,' and all that. What's the good of you and I playing a farce together, for nobody's benefit, and nothing but empty boxes in the house ? I'll tell you what it is, Pompuss. I'll do what's generous by you. I like people to do it by me, and I'll do it by you. Not half a bad tap, that Madeira. Another glass ; thank you. Now, you look here, Pompuss. If you'll make it all square and smooth with the girl, so that I sha'n't have any worry or bother over it, I'll give you a cheque on Lubbock and Robarts for five and twenty thousand pounds."

At this announcement Mr. Pompuss could not restrain his joy. He jumped up, and seized the tea dealer by the hand, shaking it as if he were going out of his mind.

" You're a trump, Sir," he cried ; " that you are. A regular trump, Sir."

" Then, that job's jobbed," said Mr. Moskins, gently, taking his hand away.

" I accept your terms. It's a bargain. The girl shall be yours."

" Is she what they call a good girl ? Church and prayers, and that ?"

" Good as gold, my dear Sir."

" All the better. If she gets into her tantarums, can always tell her to go and say her prayers. No end of a pull, that, over a girl."

" So it is," replied Pompuss.

" Well, will you make the first advances—open the ball, as one may say ?"

" Yes, you can leave all that to me."

"And you can call me in when you want me," suggested Mr. Moskins.

"All in good time, my dear Sir," answered Pompuss. "Butter's never made without churning."

"Who said it was?" demanded Mr. Moskins, sharply.

"Nobody, my dear Sir, nobody," replied Pompuss, in some alarm.

"Very well, then."

"Are you fond of singing?" asked Pompuss. "If so, Myra will give you a song."

"Will she? Come on, then," replied Mr. Moskins. ",What do you call her? Myra?"

"Pretty name, isn't it?" said the stockbroker.

"I suppose I'm an admirer—eh, Pompuss?" added Moskins, with a grin.

When they re-entered the drawing-room, Mrs. Pompuss was reading the "last prediction" of Dr. Cumming. Myra was in the abstracted state, as if she were engaged in deciding on some course of action in a difficult matter.

Mr. Moskins had drank as much wine as he could carry, and his gait was the least bit unsteady. Directly he came into the room he exclaimed—

"I hear you sing like a nightingale, Miss Myra?"

"My name is Fontaine," she said, angry at being addressed by her Christian name by a perfect stranger.

"Beg pardon, I'm sure; no offence. Will you favour us with a ditty?"

"A ditty! what's a ditty?" asked Myra, with a sort of half smile.

"Oh, you know," replied Mr. Moskins. "What the French call a chonsong; anything light and airy."

"Oh!" said Myra. "Perhaps you will give me an example."

"Well, there's—let's see—there's 'Where are you

going to, my pretty maid, my pretty maid ?' It comes in so nicely, ' My pretty maid, my pretty maid !' "

" But that's a duet !"

" Ah ! so it is. Well, there's ' Woodman, spare that tree !' "

" I will sing you that, if you wish it," replied Myra, who, confident in her own powers, never required any pressing either to sing or to play.

In a short time she found the book she wanted, and, placing it before her on the piano, sang what Mr. Moskins called " the ditty " with great force and expression. It was not exactly "light and airy," as he expressed it, but it seemed to please him immensely; and Mr. Moskins went home that evening, fancying himself deeply in love with Myra; while she, poor girl, had no more idea of the fate that her uncle contemplated for her than the man in the moon.

CHAPTER VI.

Touch and Go.

The next day Mr. Pompuss said to his niece, "Have
you thought over the little matter we were discussing
the other day at breakfast?"

Myra replied that she had.

"Very well. I told you then what my wishes were;
but I am afraid, my dear Myra, that they were a little
distasteful to you. Was it so—eh?"

"I will tell you, uncle," she replied, "what my feelings on the subject are. You asked me to marry a man
I don't care a straw about—a man I have no liking for
whatever—a man I should hate, if there was anything
worth hating about him; and can you wonder at my
feeling rebellious, and making up my mind not to do
as you wished me? You know, dear uncle," she added, as
she saw his brow darken as she said that she had resolved
to resist his wishes, "you know, I have never disobeyed
you since my father died and made you my guardian;
but in an affair of the heart I think ladies ought to
have their own way a little."

"So you shall, my dear," replied her uncle, who had
listened attentively to what she had been saying. "I
have reconsidered the matter, and I see that you cannot be happy with Sir Philip. I was only talking to your
aunt about it last night."

"Oh! that is kind of you. I felt sure that you would
never force me to marry a man against my will," said
Myra, her face brightening.

"And I have made other arrangements for you," said Mr. Pompuss, feeling his way a little cautiously, for he knew that he was treading upon dangerous ground, "other arrangements, my dear—other arrangements."

Myra looked at him inquiringly.

"You see, my dear child, you are old enough to think of being married now, and both your aunt and myself would like to see you well provided for and settled in life. You have refused a title, and perhaps you were right to do so, but it is necessary to have something in a husband—either rank, or money, or position, at any rate; something, my dear, at any rate—something; and, with your interest at heart, finding that you do not care for the advantages of rank, I looked about me to see what else I could do for you I said to myself, 'She doesn't care for that which most women think a good deal of; so I suppose she cares for money'—cares for money, my dear—eh? Was I right? Is it so—eh? Is it so?"

"No, dear uncle. You are wrong again," she replied. "Why should I care for money? I am comparatively rich; I shall never want for anything; I have something to look forward to. You know you have twenty thousand—isn't it twenty?—twenty thousand pounds my father left me, in your keeping; and when I come of age I shall have that. So why should I marry for money?"

Mr. Pompuss winced as his niece alluded to the money of which he was the custodian and trustee. He very well knew where that money was at that time, and how it was employed. Visions of certain clauses in the Fraudulent Trustees Act rose up before him, and he was afraid.

"My dear child," he replied, "you must allow one who is so much older than yourself to judge for you.

You admit, of course, that the only motive I can have in advising you is a wish to be of service to you."

" Oh, yes."

" I had hoped that someone I have lately met with would have been just the man for you."

" Who is he?" said Myra, as her heart misgave her at the turn the conversation was taking.

" He is a gentleman, possessed of immense property, and ——"

" Yes, yes," interposed Myra, impatiently; " but what is his name? Who is he? Have I seen him?"

" You have once."

" Why, uncle, you cannot mean," began Myra, laughing at the idea, " you cannot mean that man you brought home last night?"

" What nonsense you talk, Myra. Mr. Moskins ——"

" That vulgar man!" cried Myra, in astonishment.

" He is a very rich man, and would make you a very good husband." said Mr. Pompuss.

" What is his other name? Let me hear what you propose I shall change my own dear father's name for?"

" Well, there's nothing in a name."

" I think there is. What is it?"

"His name is Isaac Moskins. But fifteen or twenty thousand a-year ——"

"Mrs. Isaac Moskins! Well, upon my word!" said Myra, putting her hands together. " The man's a Jew, of course?"

" He doesn't look like it. But even if he is, he's none the worse for that, my dear—none the worse for that," replied her uncle.

" Oh, indeed!" replied Myra. " Well, I have a prejudice against being closely allied to the children of Israel. I daresay it is very silly, but I don't like the idea of it."

"Myra," said Mr. Pompuss, slowly, "think before you speak again. I want you to marry this man. It is for your interest and for mine. I must interpose my authority, if you refuse to comply with my request. If you do so, I must see what effect my command will have upon you. Your father delegated his authority to me."

"My father! Oh, do not talk of my father. He would never have wished me to make so great a sacrifice"

"Myra, my dear Myra, you will accept Mr. Moskins —eh? You will accept him, will you not?" said her uncle, in a tone of entreaty.

"It is very painful to me to refuse you anything, uncle," she replied; "but I cannot marry your friend, Mr. Moskins. Sir Philip Deverill, bad as he is, would be better, far better, than him."

"Do you refuse to marry him, then?"

"If you want to have an answer in the plainest English I know, you shall," she answered.

Mr. Pompuss said nothing, He was very pale, and his fingers moved about restlessly, almost nervously.

"I will not marry that man, uncle, even to please you," continued Myra. "I am not a child now, and I think I may please myself in taking so decided a step as that of marriage."

"There must be some reason for this," exclaimed her uncle.

It was now Myra's turn to be silent.

"What is the reason, child — eh? What is the reason?"

"Suppose I prefer a poor gentleman to a rich trades-man?" said Myra, incautiously.

"A poor gentleman," repeated Mr. Pompuss, slowly. "Oh! a poor gentleman."

Myra blushed.

"Now we come to the root of the evil," continued Mr. Pompuss. "Pray, who is this poor gentleman?"

"I won't stay here to be questioned by you," said Myra. "You have no right to question me in this way. It is very unkind of you to try and drag all my secrets out of me like this. I won't speak to you at all."

Mr. Pompuss reflected a moment or too; then he jumped up from his chair, and bringing his fist forcibly down upon the table, exclaimed—

"It's that scoundrel; I know it's that scoundrel!"

"He's no more a scoundrel than you—than you—you are," sobbed Myra, who had burst into tears.

"The villain!" said Mr. Pompuss.

"He—he's—not a v—villain," said Myra, between her sobs.

"If that's the man of your choice," said her uncle, "you shall never marry him—never. I will take care of that. So don't alarm yourself, my dear—don't alarm yourself."

"I think you are v—very c—oarse in what you—you say," replied Myra, still sobbing.

Mr. Pompuss walked excitedly up and down the room for the space of several minutes, and neither uncle nor niece exchanged a word. Then Myra got up and walked towards the door.

Mr. Pompuss seized her by the arm, and said—

"Sit down again, and listen to me."

Myra allowed herself to be reconducted to her seat, and there she sat, awaiting her uncle's pleasure.

"Myra," he said, quite calmly now—for great perils calm some men—"Myra, you love Frank Ogilvie?"

Myra made no answer.

"I see it, I see it. I must have been blind not to have noticed it before. I should have sent you miles and miles away from him—miles away from him. And you would marry a poor curate, without a halfpenny, in preference to—to—to those I have selected for you?"

Myra wept.

"Speak to me," he said.

"Oh! What can I say? You know all."

Mr. Pompuss drew his chair close to that of his niece, and he said, with considerable emotion—

"I asked you to listen to me. Will you now—will you?"

Myra nodded.

"What I am going to tell you is very painful, but the time has come when you ought to know it. I thought I should have avoided the necessity, but I can't—I can't. It is no use making a long speech, Myra. The fact is, I have been speculating with your money. There, now, you have it."

Myra smiled faintly, and replied, "Is that all, uncle? I thought you were going to tell me something much more serious."

"All! Why, God bless me! how the girl takes it! Cool as a cucumber. Isn't that enough? If anybody had told me that they had placed twenty thousand pounds of mine in jeopardy, I think I should have had a fit—had a fit. By George! yes."

"Come now, uncle; let me hear all about it. Why should this loss influence my marriage?"

"A few days ago," replied Mr. Pompuss, "I thought this money as safe as if I had put it in Exchequer Bills, or a Government Annuity; and then I wanted you to marry Sir Philip Deverill for his title. But now the whole complexion of the case is altered. I invested in Grand Trunks, thinking they would bring me in fifteen or twenty per cent.; but, instead of that, they are going all to nothing;—a complete smash, I assure you. Now, if you marry Moskins, the whole thing will come right, my dear—the whole thing will come right."

"But how?" demanded Myra, in much perplexity.

"Well, it's just this way," replied her uncle, "just this way. You see, I have a private understanding with

Moskins that, if you marry him, he is to give me a good many thousand pounds; and then I can pay you back, and it will be all right once more."

"What?" said Myra, her eyes flashing, and her frame trembling.

"Oh! don't be frightened. He won't miss it—won't miss it. The man's as rich as a Jew."

Myra took no notice of his exculpation. She said, in an agony of rage—

"You dared to drive a bargain in this way?"

"Drive a bargain!"

"You dared to sell me to a wretch like that? Oh! why am I thrown amongst such men?"

"Now, don't, Myra, don't," said Mr. Pompuss, soothingly, "don't take on like that. What's the good? There's no harm done."

"Go on," she said, "go on, if you have anything else to say."

Tears of passion started to her eyes, and her face was as red as fire.

"You see, my dear Myra," he continued, thinking that because she was quiet she was likely to fall into his views, "you see, if you go and marry this parson fellow—marry this parson fellow —— "

Myra started, but she clenched her hands together, murmuring to herself—

"What else can I expect, what else can I look for, from such people? If my poor father had only lived!"

"He would look to me for your twenty thousand, and I should not be able to give it him, because it's all sunk in Grand Trunks."

The pitiable expression of Mr. Pompuss's face as he said this was ludicrous. Myra would have laughed at it had she not been too miserable. Myra said nothing.

"You, my dear," he continued, " don't know the value of money; but a twopenny-halfpenny curate, who has never had more than five pounds to spend at a time in his life, would look uncommonly sharp after the pounds, shillings, and pence, for which I am accountable to you—accountable to you; and he would show me no mercy. As a religious man, he would, perhaps, feel it his duty—these fellows always stand upon duty —his duty to prosecute me."

" Do what, uncle ?" cried Myra.

" Why, prosecute me, my dear. Have me up at the Central Criminal, and send me across the Herringpond for the term of my natural life—term of my natural life. That's how they express it, I think."

" Is it so serious as that ?" said Myra, rather touched.

"I'm not exaggerating a bit, my dear—not a bit," he replied, eagerly.

" Oh, but he would not do such a thing "

" Can't say that ; can't say that. He might, you know, and probably would. You must admit there is the possibility."

" It is a very slender one, though," said Myra.

" Slender or not, my dear, there it is ; and if the curate took such an idea in his head, would you not feel bound to sacrifice your uncle to your husband? He would back himself up by all the texts in the Bible."

Myra could not answer this argument.

" You would not like to see me a felon, Myra ; would you, eh ?—would you ?" said her uncle, looking at her with all the earnestness he could command.

He certainly felt what he said, and Myra could not help being penetrated with compassion at his evident and palpable distress.

" Do not talk of such dreadful things, dear uncle," she said, kindly laying her hand upon his arm. " I would do anything in reason to save you from any unpleasantness."

"You would marry Moskins, eh ?—marry Moskins ?" he exclaimed.

"Oh, no, no! Anything but that."

"But to save me?"

"No; not even to save you," replied Myra, tear-fully, but firmly.

"Then, there is but one thing left," said Mr. Pompuss, rising from his seat, and going towards a small writing-case, which contained some private papers of his. Opening this desk, he took out a small phial. It was labelled "Prussic Acid." Myra followed all his movements with great and undisguised curiosity. Holding up the phial, he exclaimed, "I cannot live to be disgraced, Myra. This acid causes death in less than a minute after it has passed one's lips. I have only one regret in dying—only one regret; and that is, that my niece, whom I always loved, should drive me into a premature grave. Take care of and comfort your aunt, Myra; will you? It is my last request."

His hand trembled a little as he raised the phial to his lips; but Myra, who had been changing colour like a chameleon during this strange scene, rushed forward, and, with the quickness of lightning, dashed the bottle from his hand. It fell with a crash against the wall, and broke. A strong smell of bitter almonds impregnated the atmosphere, and filled the room.

Myra's lips were bleeding in one or two places. She had bitten them severely. Her agitation had evidently been excessive; but she said, with great calmness—

"You must not die like that; you must live. I—I will m—marry your friend."

"God bless you, Myra! God ——" began Mr. Pompuss. But when he looked round to thank her, she had vanished from the room. If he had listened, he might have heard her murmuring, as she went—

"Oh, how hard it is to go to heaven! It is, indeed, a hard and narrow path. Duty and inclination are always at war with each other; but there was One who suffered much, and never murmured. May I, oh! may I be like Him!"

Mr. Pompuss sat down in an arm-chair, and wiped the thick drops of perspiration from his forehead.

"I have conquered," he said, "but it was touch and go, Sir—touch and go."

CHAPTER VII.

FRANK OGILVIE.

FRANK OGILVIE was sitting in his room, as he might have done a few years before at Trinity. He was reading Horace. Sometimes he allowed himself the luxury of a couple of Odes, or some peculiarly brilliant lines in his favourite Satires. But this was only when he thought he had deserved well of himself. He worked very hard, for he was a conscientious labourer in the vineyard. One hope, one thought, one prospect, however, cheered him up in the midst of his severest toil; and that was, that some day or other he firmly believed Myra Fontaine would be his wife. The very good and holy, the very pure and simple-minded have an exalted idea of matrimony, much more so than the herd of worldlings, who rush blindly into it, and soon after apply to Sir James Plaisted Wilde to rid them of an encumbrance they never ought to have charged themselves with. Ogilvie was one of those men who, when they once allow themselves to love, love for ever. They are as fond and darling at forty as they are at twenty. He had met Myra Fontaine soon after taking orders, and although no positive pledges had passed between them, it was tacitly understood between them that they were to be man and wife.

A scene had once taken place between Ogilvie and Mr. Pompuss. The latter had an idea of what actually was taking place in his house; but he was not certain. One day he surprised the lovers together. He loaded

Ogilvie with insults, and ordered him out of his house. Ogilvie did not in the least lose his temper ; he merely replied —

"It is true, I love your niece. I am not aware that I am doing anything wrong in cherishing a passion for the most beautiful woman I ever dreamed of. You have insulted me very grossly, but my consolation is, that your knowledge of my profession has emboldened you to do so ; for, were I not a priest, you would scarcely dare to treat me as you have done. I may tell you frankly, before I leave your house, that I shall continue to love your niece ; and if she is willing to marry me when she is of age, I shall not consider that you have any right to prevent my leading her to the altar."

"Out of my house, Sir—out of my house," was all Mr. Pompuss could say to this address, which was as mild and temperate and gentlemanly as any man could have made it.

After this, Myra and Ogilvie met frequently, not exactly clandestinely ; for they made no secret of it. But the curate did not call upon her at her home ; he met her at the Sunday-school, or the Day-school, or after service sometimes.

Frank Ogilvie was just reading "O matre pulchra filia pulchrior," when the door of his room opened, and the servant of the house he lodged in said—

"Please, Sir, there's a young lady, Sir, as wishes to see you, Sir."

"A young lady ! Do you know her name ?"

"No, Sir ; but she giv' me this."

Ogilvie took the card the servant held in her dirty hand, and read the name written upon it. He changed colour, and said quickly—

"Just be good enough to ask the lady to come up, will you ?"

In a short time the door opened a second time, and Myra Fontaine entered.

The curate offered her a chair, and shook her hand warmly, saying—

"How kind of you! I am really so glad to see you."

Myra's hand lay in his, motionless. It was cold, almost pulseless. Her countenance was stony and impassive; at times a nervous twitch passed over it, and there was a movement in her throat as if she would have given the world to cry, or as if she had been crying bitterly, and was still a little hysterical. She had worn a thick Maltese veil, but she lifted it up as she came in.

As Ogilvie noticed all these circumstances, he said hurriedly—

"What is the matter, dear Myra? Are you ill? Has anything happened?"

Myra tried to speak, but after two or three efforts, she sat down on the chair he had given her, and burst into a flood of tears.

Ogilvie ran into his bedroom and brought out some salts and some Eau-de-Cologne, and after a time succeeded in calming her. When the paroxysm was past she said, in a voice broken by hysterical sobs—

"Oh! Frank, Frank! How shall I ever tell you?"

"Tell me! Tell me what?" replied Ogilvie. "Oh! what has happened? For God's sake, let me know at once. Is it that you do not love me? You have changed your mind, or you have met someone you like better?"

Myra raised her eyes, which were swollen with weeping, and looked at him reproachfully. Her lips moved, as she said, in a faint voice, so faint as to be hardly audible—

"I love you, but I can never be your wife."

He threw himself on his knees by her side; he caught hold of one of her hands, and smothered it with kisses; then, remembering where he was, and what she had just said, he sprang up, and sat, cold and formal and rigid, in his arm-chair. He had given her his last caress; it was the offspring of despair.

"I will tell you all," began Myra, "and then you shall sit in judgment upon me."

"No, Myra; tell me nothing," he replied, sadly. "I know you so well that I am convinced you have acted for the best. I do not wish to know by what circumstances or in what way you are influenced. You have told me you love me; that is sufficient for me. I love you, God alone knows how much. You love me. That declaration will sustain me. Knowing that I possess your love, I can die happy."

"Oh! do let me explain. I am not to blame; indeed, I am not," said Myra.

Ogilvie seemed cut out of stone; he did not move a muscle. He was like a beautiful statue.

Myra, thinking that his silence indicated consent, told him the events that had happened when she prevented her uncle from poisoning himself, and subsequently pledged him her word that she would marry Mr. Isaac Moskins.

He listened to her almost as if he heard her not; but, when she had finished, he said—

"I have often preached resignation to others, but I never till now knew how hard adversity was to bear."

"But I love you, and you only!" exclaimed Myra.

"For pity's sake, do not say that again, or you will drive me mad," he cried.

Then there was a pause.

"I did think once that, with you, I should almost realize the idea of heaven upon earth," he said, in that sort of voice that a man uses when his heart is broken, or when he is thoroughly worn-out and beaten by adverse fates.

Myra's cheek was blanched, and she looked as if she had committed some crime, and was being arraigned for it.

"What could I do?" she said, plaintively; "what *could* I do?"

"Leave me now, Myra," he replied. "I will not blame you for seeking this interview; but it would have been kinder, perhaps, to have stayed away."

"Oh! don't say that, Frank. Do not speak unkindly to me *now*," she said.

"Good-bye, Myra. I will pray for your happiness."

She advanced towards him, as if she would shake his hand; but he drew back, almost shrinkingly, and said—

"No, no. It is better not. Please, leave me. I may be calmer next time we meet. God bless you, Myra!"

He averted his eyes, and Myra tottered, rather than walked, from the room. When she had gone, and the door had closed upon her retreating figure, Frank Ogilvie moistened the floor with his tears. It was a feminine weakness, but he could not help it; he was utterly prostrated. He might have continued an hour or more like this, when he rallied a little, and, clasping his hands, said in a low tone—

"She might have come between my God and me. His will be done."

CHAPTER VIII.

"Arimanes had a Talisman; so have I."

The position of Grand Trunks of Bohemia grew worse and worse day by day. All the holders of the ill-omened stock rushed in to sell, and the predictions of Sir Philip Deverill were more than confirmed. When the news that the Government refused to ratify the sale of the land was received at Capel-court, the jobbers would not make a price for more than three minutes together. There were a few rich holders who rushed in to buy after the depreciation, but even they could not arrest the downward movement; for numbers of speculators, who could not possibly deliver the stock, went in and sold Bears of them. These men saw the downward movement, and went in for their one or two per cent., which having achieved, they instantly closed their accounts, and went home happy in the consciousness of having made their twenty or thirty pounds.

Mr. Isaac Moskins, alarmed at the reports which reached him from various quarters, sought the office of his broker, and determined to close his account at a loss, if the rumours which he had heard received further confirmation in a continued depreciation in the value of Grand Trunk scrip.

Mr. Pompuss was not looking much at his ease. He was busily engaged in calculating the per-centage on certain stocks, as settling-day was close at hand, and he had been requested by his clients to carry over.

"Morning, Pompuss!" exclaimed Mr. Moskins, as he entered the office.

E

"Ah! Hope I see you well," replied the broker, making an entry in a book.

"Can I speak a word to you?"

"Certainly. Step this way," said Mr. Pompuss.

He led his client into his private room, and shut to the door.

It was about twelve o'clock, and the day of the week was Saturday.

"Have you the last prices?" asked Mr. Moskins.

"No, I have not, within a quarter of an hour. But I will run and get them for you."

"Never mind; that's near enough. How are the markets to-day?"

"Oh! markets are good. Consols come an eighth better," replied the broker.

"I am almost afraid to ask how Trunks are," said Mr. Moskins.

"Trunks are the only bad thing in the market. They're quoted seventeen, twenty. All sellers, no buyers."

"God bless me!" cried Mr. Moskins. "What do they say of them?"

"Nothing good, I am sorry to say. Truth is, I sold mine this morning early at sixteen. Frightful loss; but didn't like to hold on."

"D) you think they'll go much lower?" asked Moskins.

"Really, can't say; impossible to say. Queer sort of market," replied Mr. Pompuss.

"If it wasn't bad business to sell after so heavy a fall, I should say to you, Pompuss, go in and sell fifty thousand."

"Well, they are all Bears; every man Jack of them. All Bears, Sir. There isn't a Bull in the market; and I think that has something to do with the fall."

Mr. Isaac Moskins thought a little, and said—

"I'll tell you what it is. I'm in for a loss; that there is no question about. And you're bitten, too, as hard as I am."

"Yes, I'm hard hit enough," answered Mr. Pompuss, with a sigh.

"Well, now, you go in, and close my account, and sell ten thousand for this account."

"You won't do them for next month?"

"No; this account. And when you're there, see what you will have to give for the put of Consols."

"Put of Consols! Heard anything lately — any news?" asked Mr. Pompuss.

"Well, there's something in the wind; but I don't exactly know what," replied Mr. Moskins.

"Anything else I can do for you?" inquired the broker.

"You are going to carry over my Consolides?"

"Yes; but they ask rather a high price for doing it. I daresay I shall have to pay ten per cent."

"Indeed!"

"I think it's a good thing to do though; there'll be a rise in that stock, Sir—a rise in that stock," replied Mr. Pompuss.

When Mr. Isaac Moskins saw his orders punctually and faithfully attended to, he went over to Mincing-lane to see some friends of his, and to show himself like a Triton amongst the minnows.

Mr. Pompuss was busily engaged in reckoning up his losses in Grand Trunks, which he discovered, much to his disgust, had swallowed up eighteen thousand pounds out of the twenty he had put on them. He had, therefore, defrauded. Yes, "defrauded" was the word; and, do what he could, his conscience would not allow him to shirk it. He had defrauded his niece, Myra Fontaine, of her fortune, or, at least, the best part of it. He had the figures pretty nearly at his fingers' ends; but, in

E 2

order to confirm some small items, he put his hand in his pocket for his private memorandum-book. He felt first in one pocket, and then in another, without finding it. He got as hot as fire, and went through all the pleasures of a Turkish bath except the shampooing process, without paying a halfpenny for it; for he got hot and cold, and then very warm, and then uncommonly chilly. His memorandum-book contained all his secrets; in it he had put down everything relating to Myra's fortune, and how he had expended it. It contained notes of all his time bargains. He would not have lost that book for much more than a thousand pounds.

"Well, that's like my luck lately," he said, half aloud. "Suppose that confounded book falls into the hands of some clever fellow. Why, his fortune's made. He can work me to any extent. Curse the luck! Curse it—curse it!"

In the midst of his objurgations, one of his clerks opened the door, peeped in, and said—

"Sir Philip Deverill, Sir. Tell him you're busy, Sir; or will you see him?"

"Ask him to walk in," replied Mr. Pompuss.

When Sir Philip made his appearance, the broker said—

"Take a chair. Anything I can do for you this morning? Rather busy. Markets good; Trunks very bad—very bad indeed. Funds good. French Funds come a little better. Just got the telegram. Fifteen centimes. Credit Mobilier and Credit Foncier, all good. Anything I can do for you this morning? Rather busy."

And Mr. Pompuss looked down on his paper, and went on making up his accounts, and cursing the loss of his pocket-book.

"I am sorry to trouble you, Pompuss; but I want a little private conversation with you this morning, parti-

cularly," said Sir Philip. He laid a stress upon the word
" particularly."

" Can't spare a minute this morning. Making up
day, you know. Up to my neck in business, as a man
may say," replied the broker. " Any other day. Be
only too glad. Anything I can do for you ?"

" Well, no. I don't want you to buy or sell, or carry
over for me ; but yet I want to talk to you," replied the
baronet.

Mr. Pompuss looked up in astonishment at his
visitor's pertinacity.

Seeing that he had arrested his attention, Sir Philip
said—

" I hope your charming niece is well ?"

" Quite well, I thank you—quite well."

" I had the pleasure of calling at your house just
now."

" Indeed !"

" Miss Fontaine was not visible ; but I had the
pleasure of seeing your wife, and from her I heard
something about a marriage being on the *tapis* between
your niece and a Mr. Isaac Moskins ; and I have just
looked in to see if there is any truth in the report."

The broker was a good deal taken aback at this plain
question, so plainly put. He hardly knew how to reply
to it. He had tacitly encouraged Sir Philip's advances,
and he felt that he had been acting in bad faith in
throwing him over in favour of a richer suitor.

" Young ladies, Sir Philip, as I daresay you know,
must please themselves," he replied, with a smile.

" I ask you a plain question ; will you be good
enough to give me a plain answer ?" said the baronet.

Mr. Pompuss looked annoyed at this, and said
abruptly—

" Yes, there is. Good morning. I'm sure you'll
excuse me ; but I am very busy."

Sir Philip Deverill did not attempt to move. He sat with one hand in the pocket of his coat, as if it was clasping som·thing. The stockbroker went on with his accounts, without taking any further notice of the baronet. But when, after the lapse of a quarter of a minute, he saw that he still sat there, he touched a little alarum which stood upon the table. The clear, bell-like ring sounded through the office.

" Why do you ring?" asked Sir Philip.

"I thought you either did not know, or had forgotten, your way out," Mr. Pompuss replied.

" Neither one nor the other, my dear Pompuss," returned the baronet, blandly. "I was merely collecting my thoughts, and allowing you to finish your arithmetical puzzles. The fact is, I have something to tell you and to talk about which will not brook the slightest del y."

"And that is ——"

" Well, send your clerk away, and you shall hear."

Mr Pompuss turned to the clerk, who had answered his summons, and said—

" Has any one been from Hankey's?"

" No, Sir," replied the clerk, and withdrew,

"Very well done, my dear Pompuss," said Sir Philip. "I did not know you were so good a tactician. But, now we are alone once more, we can proceed to business."

" Well, go on," said the broker, impatiently, biting the end of his pen as he spoke.

" Your niece has a fortune of twenty thousand pounds, I believe?"

" Well, suppose she has?"

" Supposition, my dear Pompuss, is of very little use to a business man. I had an idea that such was the fact; but I went to Doctors' Commons, and paid a shilling to see the late Mr. Fontaine's will; and I found that such was the fact, and that you were the sole executor."

"Yes, that's right enough."

" I know it is, my dear Pompuss. It is not necessary for you to give me that assurance, since I have seen it, in black and white, with my own eyes."

" It's a nice little fortune, a tidy little sum, for a man without a rap, isn't it ?" sneered Mr. Pompuss, who was getting angry at being interrupted and stuck to by his visitor.

"So I was thinking, my dear fellow," replied the baronet. "I said to myself, 'Deverill, you are not a rich man ; you are far from being a rich man, or from having any hopes of becoming a rich man. Now, twenty thousand pounds to a clever man like yourself would be a great acquisition. Why, in twelve months you would very nearly double it. Think of that. Double it ! And if, in addition to that, you can get a beautiful wife, you will most assuredly be in luck's way. Now, Myra Fontaine is beautiful, and she has twenty thousand pounds. What can possibly be better for you than to marry Myra Fontaine ? Nothing—clearly nothing. *Eh, bien !*' There are the premises, and there is the inference fairly deduced from them."

" You will never marry my niece !" cried Mr. Pompuss, passionately ; " and if you have only come here to talk such dire nonsense to me, Sir Philip, the sooner you leave my office the better. I have given you more than one hint in a gentlemanly way."

"Gentlemanly !" echoed Sir Philip, sarcastically.

"And you have refused to take it. I now tell you that I am engaged, and that I shall feel relieved by your absence."

" That I have no doubt of," replied the baronet, " not the least in the world. But I have not the slightest intention of going just yet, my dear Pompuss ; not the slightest, I assure you."

" My clerks will —— "

"No, they won't, Pompuss," said Sir Philip; "not a bit of it. Did you ever hear of Arimanes?"

Mr. Pompuss shook his head.

" Oh, you didn't. Well, Arimanes had a talisman; so have I."

Sir Philip put his hand in his pocket. The stockbroker looked perplexed, and awaited the sequel in silence.

CHAPTER IX.

TIRED OF HIS LIFE.

SIR PHILIP DEVERILL looked carefully round the
room, as if apprehensive of some interruption. His
scrutiny seemed to be only partially satisfactory, for he
said—

"I suppose, no one can overhear what I am going
to say to you, Pompuss ? Not that I care particularly;
only you may object to your clerks listening to our
private affairs."

The phrase, "our private affairs," seemed to attract
the stockbroker's attention. It was singular that the
baronet should make use of a word which showed that
their interests were not as antagonistic as he had at
first supposed. If that was the case, he had little or
nothing to dread, although at first, from Sir Philip's
manner, Mr. Pompuss had feared that something of an
unpleasant nature was about to happen to him. Nor
were his presentiments so false as to have much misled
him.

The broker assured Sir Philip that there was no
chance of their conversation being heard by anybody.
"This is my private room," he said; "I often transact
matters here of the greatest importance. It is not
likely, as such is the case, that I should choose a room
where anybody who chooses, or has the opportunity,
to listen could avail himself of it to my prejudice."

"I think all things are fair in love and war," began
the baronet, "and bearing this adage in my mind, I

have not scrupled to use weapons which, strictly speaking, are hardly admissible in honourable warfare."

" Honourable warfare! What on earth do you mean— on earth do you mean, eh ?" said Pompuss. "Really, you are going in for riddles. If you have anything to say, let me beg of you to say it at once."

" Riddles—eh ? They may seem so to you; but I will soon make it all clear to you. Suppose, now, I were to say to you, Pompuss, you are not the man of honour people generally suppose you to be; you ——"

" Who dare say such a thing ?" cried Mr. Pompuss, rising, indignantly.

" Don't excite yourself. Sit down again. I am coming to it all in good time. Where was I ? You have put me out. Oh! Suppose I were to say to you, Pompuss, you are a rogue, a swindler, a ——"

Mr. Pompuss took up an inkstand, and, without hesitation, hurled it at Sir Philip's head; but the baronet, seeing the missile coming, bowed his head, and it struck the wall behind him. The ink flew about in all directions, and did not at all improve the pattern of the paper.

" Now, see what you have done, my good Pompuss. If you had only been quiet, you would not have spoilt your paper. It is a great pity men will not learn to command their tempers."

" You—you must explain this," stammered Mr. Pompuss, in a voice almost inarticulate from rage.

" With pleasure," replied the baronet. " Such language as I have just made use of should not be employed between one gentleman and another without some very good and excellent reason. Now, I have a very good reason indeed—couldn't be more so. I think I was making use of a very disagreeable epithet when you interrupted me. I called you, in a suppositionary manner, a rogue—I was going on to say *a fraudulent trustee.*"

" Wh—what ?" gasped the stockbroker, turning ashy pale, and crumbling up in his hand the blotting-paper which lay on the desk before him.

" That goes home, does it ?" said Sir Philip. " Hard hit—eh ?" And he laughed a quiet laugh of triumph, as much as to say, " That man is in my power. I can do with him as I list. I can crush him at will, or twist him round my finger like a ball of thread. He is mine as much as if I were the devil, and he had sold his soul to me."

Mr. Pompuss seemed completely prostrated by this sudden and unexpected declaration. Innumerable thoughts flashed across his mind, but he could hardly think that Sir Philip Deverill had any confirmation of what he said. Mr. Pompuss's idea of the matter was, that the baronet had, in some inexplicable manner, obtained some slight information which gave rise to a suspicion gradually developing into the serious charge he had just brought against him. It would be better, he considered, to deny it altogether, and brazen it out. " Perhaps, if I remain firm, it will choke him off, and I shall once more have the field to myself." Sir Philip's taunts had the effect also of encouraging him, and he replied to his accusation, boldly and angrily—

" What you say, Sir, is a lie—a lie! Do you hear me ? A lie !"

" A lie, is it ? Well, I don't think so," replied Sir Philip, coolly. " Do you ever make notes, Pompuss ?"

" Occasionally."

" In a pocket-book ?"

Sir Philip said this slowly, laying a stress upon every word, and looking fixedly upon his victim.

The effect of this speech upon the stockbroker was very marked indeed. His former air of defiance changed to one of abject fear. He looked perfectly bewildered, and, in a craven, cowed sort of manner, he went up to Sir Philip, and said—

" You have found it ?"

" Well, I don't mind acknowledging that I have."

The broker stood before this man like a schoolboy who expects to have a theme or a copy of verses torn over. He did not utter a word; he only looked ill and harassed, and intensely anxious.

Sir Philip's demeanour was more determined than ever, and he had the appearance of a man who was about to drive a hard bargain with a poor devil who couldn't help himself.

" In this pocket-book of yours, Pompuss, which I had the good fortune to pick up on your drawing-room carpet this morning, when I called upon you, I have found several entries respecting the investment of twenty thousand pounds belonging to your niece, Myra Fontaine. Your notes state that you invested this sum in the Grand Trunk Railway of Bohemia, the shares of which undertaking are this morning scarcely worth the paper they are written upon. This being the case, it follows that you have speculated with your niece's money, and lost it. I know enough of your affairs to tell that you have no possibility of replacing this money. Therefore, you are in a mess. Do you understand me ? Shall I reduce it to a syllogism for you? Oh, you understand me well enough—very well. Now, did you ever hear of the Fraudulent Trustees Act ? I think it passed in '56 or '58. Never mind the date. You never read it ? Well, you will probably become more acquainted with its provisions at some future day All I have to do now is to hint to you that it can bring you to the Old Bailey any day as a fraudulent trustee."

Mr. Pompuss, during this harangue, had looked very crestfallen, but of a sudden a gleam of hope irradiated his countenance, and he exclaimed—

" You want a couple of thousand or so—eh ? I have still a little left at my bankers. It isn't much, perhaps hardly worth your acceptance—hardly worth it; if it is, I will write you a cheque at once."

"I don't want to send you to the Old Bailey, Pompuss," said Sir Philip, pleasantly; "but are you aware, my dear fellow, that you are aggravating your offence by trying to compound a felony? Oh, you didn't know. Well, you know it now? You are far too nice a fellow to mix with the aborigines of Australia, and light your pipe with your ticket-of-leave after having dined substantially on damper and kangaroo-tail soup. You are worthy of better things, Pompuss. The Roupell sort of game is all very well in its way, but it is not much to my mind, and I don't think you have any more fancy for it than I have. If you have, why, you are not the clever fellow I take you for."

"What do you want, then?" said Pompuss. "You don't want money. What is it that you do want; for you must have some end in view? For heaven's sake, cut it short, and put me out of my misery."

"Cut it short!" cried Sir Philip Deverill. "There is an elegant expression to come from a City man, and a stockbroker too."

"Will you come to the point?" replied Mr. Pompuss, imploringly.

"To oblige you, I will. There are some things that men care for more than for money. Now, there is an object which I have set my heart on achieving, and that is an alliance with the noble house of Pompuss. The fact is, I want your niece."

"Confound the girl! I wish she had never been born," said the stockbroker. "I have had nothing but trouble and worry with her. First I speculate with her money, and lose it for her; then Moskins wants her, and I've promised him that he shall have her; and then there's that curate. Why, he glares at me whenever I see him as if he wished he were a tiger, and could have a good spring at me, Sir—have a good spring at me."

"What is the arrangement between you and Moskins —eh?" asked Sir Philip. "I suppose he is to give you a certain sum of money if the event comes off—enough to put you right as regards the girl's fortune, and perhaps a thousand or so over."

Mr. Pompuss nodded.

"Well, look here. The girl herself will never make a fuss about her fortune. I, her husband, will undertake to hold you harmless; and there you are. There is a practical solution of your difficulty at once. It's no use talking, Pompuss; but I must marry that girl. I would rather have had her with the money, of course; but, if it is gone, why. there is an end of it. But have her I must. So you have only one course open to you; and that is, to back me up, and let Moskins go to the wall. Come now, it isn't so bad, after all. A gentleman's better than a tradesman any day, isn't he?"

The stockbroker saw that he was completely in the power of the man before him; so, in pugilistic language, he threw the sponge up, and knocked under to irresistible fate.

"I will do all I can for you with the girl," he said, "and Moskins shall go to the wall. You shall have my moral support, if it is worth anything to you—worth anything to you. But you will have no objection to give me a guarantee ——"

"No; you must take my word. I can give you nothing else," replied the baronet.

Mr. Pompuss thought of the maxim that beggars should not be choosers, and was silent.

Sir Philip Deverill took up his hat, and placed it jauntily on his head, saying—

"We are good friends, remember, only so long as you keep your faith with me. Once attempt to play me false, and I let slip the dogs of war. Good-bye, Pompuss. I shall call upon you this evening, when I shall look for more smiles than frowns. Now go, like a good boy, and attend to your business, or you will lose all your clients. Ta, ta!"

And the baronet sailed gaily out of the room.

"I wish to God there were such things as earthquakes in England," muttered Mr. Pompuss, "and one would happen just now, and swallow that fellow up; yes, and me, too—both of us; for I am tired of my life—tired of my life!"

CHAPTER X.

A Practical Solution of a Difficulty.

John Pompuss might well wish that he were dead, for he had involved himself in endless complications. Owing to the power that a knowledge of his guilt gave him, he was the slave of Sir Philip Deverill, as much as if he had been bound hand and foot and placed in a dungeon, or as if he had been sold at public auction in Charleston as a full-grown, able-bodied mulatto. In order to extricate himself from his difficulty, he had pledged himself to Isaac Moskins, who fully believed himself the happy man, and was constantly thinking of asking his lady-love, as he called her in his tender moments, to fix the day. Had John Pompuss been free to act, he would have said, boldly and honestly, "My niece shall marry who she likes. I will not dictate to her, although I may advise her, on such a subject." But he had fraudulently made away with Myra's fortune; and so he was a malefactor, although he had not yet been gibbeted before the public gaze. His knowledge of the law was slight, but what little legal acumen he possessed enabled him to see that Sir Philip Deverill, as the next friend—if he chose to make himself so—of Myra Fontaine, could institute an inquiry into his investment of the money of which he was the guardian and trustee. He fancied he saw her father rising from his grave and standing before him in his ghastly cerements, saying, in a voice as awful as the tomb from which he had just emerged, "Render me an account of the moneys I intrusted to your care, whereof my daughter was to have the usufruct, or, peradventure, great wrath will come upon you." The picture, whichever way he looked at it, was not a pleasant one, and John Pompuss was only too glad when business was over, and he could get into his omnibus and go homewards. The moil and toil of his every-day work being over, he could turn his attention from time bargains, and bank-rates, and short bills, puts, calls, contangos, French Funds, Consols, Grand Trunks, and all the other monetary items which were continually elbowing one another in order to have free passage through his overloaded brain. I do not know whether it has been said, but, whether or no, I will take upon myself to declare, that a man is never so much alone as when he is in an omnibus. Although it may be full of men, you are not of them or with them ; and, huddled up in your corner at the extreme end, you may let your thoughts run riot without fear of check, or let, or hindrance. This John Pompuss did, and he had not proceeded more than half-way to Highgate before a thought entered his head, and, before it could complete its passage through his cranium, he seized it and held it fast. It was of some value to him, for it showed him a loop-hole through which he could escape from his present difficulty.

"If," he argued, with a smile of triumph, "if I can persuade Moskins to advance me twenty thousand pounds down on the nail, I can pay it in to my bankers in Myra's name ; and there is an end of Sir Philip's criminal charge. He may denounce me if he chooses ; but with what result? There will be the money as safe as a church. I can reply that I do not understand the meaning of his charges. There is the money. What more can the most intimate friend of my niece require? Perhaps, if I tell Moskins that he shall marry Myra to-morrow morning, he will snap at the bait and give me

F

the money. I will try it, anyhow—I will try it. I can only fail ; and if I succeed, I shall feel that I am an honest man once more, and can look Sir Philip Deverill or any one else in the face. I'll do it, Sir—I'll do it."

No sooner was this thought practically considered than John Pompuss felt that it was his only chance. How slowly the omnibus rolled along now, when he was panting for action ! Each stoppage drove him mad. So he got out and hailed a Hansom cab, and was soon going swiftly towards his home. When he arrived there, he sought Myra, and, in a few words, asked her if she objected to her marriage with Mr. Moskins taking place immediately.

" What are you in so great a hurry for ?" she asked. " Cannot the affair be managed with common decency ?"

" Circumstances have transpired," he replied, " which render it absolutely necessary, my dear—absolutely necessary—that the ceremony should take place at once. I know how painful it is to you, but it is no less so to me. I shall be in the hands of an unscrupulous scoundrel, who has discovered my secret, and he will always have the greatest power over me. You would not like to see me dragged off to gaol, would you ? Dragged off to gaol—eh ?"

This was an appeal *ad misericordiam*. John Pompuss had tried it before, and it had succeeded ; but now it had only the effect of disgusting Myra.

" There, for Heaven's sake, do not go on canting in that way. I have given you my word, I will marry your tea-dealing friend. Isn't that enough for you ?"

" But will you, to-morrow ?" persisted her uncle, nothing abashed. "Shall I tell him that I am authorized to say so ?"

" As well to-morrow as a month hence," she replied, with a reckless laugh. " I suppose, like a wretch con- demned to be broken on the wheel, I should only shudder as I counted the hours which had to elapse

before my execution. Tell him what you like; I shall
be ready."

Mr. Pompuss was about to thank her, but she waved
her hand, as if to check him, and glided away like a
ghost.

Whe she h ad gone, Pompuss said to himself—
"Now to see Moskins. I have no time to lose. The
thing must be done quickly, if it is to be done at all;
done quickly." And, muttering to himself, "Done
quickly," he got into his cab, which he had kept
waiting, and drove to the private house of Mr. Moskins.

It was a small house in Berkeley-square; just such a
house as a bachelor would choose to live in. There were
not many rooms, but what there were, were richly
furnished, and as much with an eye to comfort as to
elegance.

When Isaac Moskins heard the stockbroker's news,
he was overpowered with joy. He happened to be at
dinner, and he persuaded his visitor to sit down and
join him. The affair was discussed *à la fourchette*, and
when John Pompuss left the house, he carried a cheque
for twenty thousand pounds with him. What did he
care for Myra, or her feelings, or her sufferings? He
had managed to get his neck out of the halter, and now
he could breathe again. He could hold up his head on
'Change, and go about without a sickening dread of
being denounced to a gaping crowd. What was the
happiness or the misery of one woman to him in com-
parison with these great benefits which he had so unex-
pectedly gained? He could laugh at Grand Trunks
now. They might go to zero if they liked; he didn't care.
And when he got home he uncorked a bottle of Madeira,
and, as he sipped its generous contents, he told his wife
"to let Doctor Cumming alone for an hour, and bustle
about to make preparations for Myra's wedding, as Mr.
Isaac Moskins was coming to claim his bride at half-past
ten to-morrow morning."   F 2

CHAPTER XI.

Mr. Moskins claims his Bride.

On the morning of the 15th of October—which was a day to be marked with black, the blackest, chalk—Myra arranged herself for the wedding as she would have done for a sacrifice. With the stolid indifference of a Suttee, she set about the work of adornment. There was not the religious fanaticism of the Hindoo devotee, but she seemed equally callous to pain and the miserable prospect before her. It was a cold, foggy morning. The first frost of winter had taken place the night before, and at Highgate the air was cold and wintry. The atmosphere seemed to have collected itself into one huge bridal veil, to hide therewith the iniquity that that day was to witness. I say iniquity, advisedly; for what can be more miserable, more wretched, more wicked, than to unite a young, lovely, accomplished, and amiable girl, who has all the world before her, to a man—well, to a man, the best you can say of whom is that he is a man, and not a gorilla?

It was a melancholy wedding. The sacred rites were to be solemnized in a very different manner to that which Myra had dreamed of when she fondly thought that she would be the bride of Frank Ogilvie. As she thought of him, it was odd that she did not weep ; it would have been better for her if she could have done so. But she was feverish and restless, and there was a strange light in her inflamed eyes. She was irritable and impatient with her maid, and angry with the man who came to dress her hair. Of course, there were to be no bridesmaids. Who of her acquaintances would consent to appear at a wedding at so short a notice? The dresses would not be made in time. Even a Regent-street dressmaker, with all her slave-driving and killing propensities, could not have got a bridal costume ready at six or ten hours' notice. So Myra made up her mind to go alone. Besides, she rather wished it. She said to herself, " I should not like any one to witness my shame. My friends would come, and be polite, and friendly, and do all the conventional things which the occasion would exact from them ; but they would despise me in their hearts."

Myra was only a child in the ways of the world, and she did not know that there are very few young ladies who will reject a rich husband when he honours them so far as to make them a proposal. Myra's costume had been hastily procured for her early in the morning by her uncle, who had taken a cab and driven to various shops to obtain what she wanted. The things were bought ready-made ; but Myra's heart was too full to take much notice of these trifles.

At the appointed hour Mr. Isaac Moskins drove up to the house in a handsome carriage and pair. The footman let down the steps with a clatter, and the tea dealer was soon in the house of the broker, who had taken a holiday for the occasion.

Mr. Moskins wished to see Myra. He said—

" Would they have the kindness to ask her to step down stairs ?"

Myra, obedient to the summons, suspended the 'tiring operations, and went down to the room in which her future husband was expecting her. She had her wedding-dress on, but her wreath was not yet placed on her head, as her hair was not finished to the satisfac-

tion of the *coiffeur*. She did not blush when she saw
Mr. Moskins; she turned a shade paler, if possible.

Moskins met her half way, and said—

"My dear girl, sit down here. I want to have five
minutes' conversation with you."

Myra took the seat he offered her, and sat with
her hands folded, looking steadily in his face. There
was a vacant look about her eyes, though, which seemed
to say, "You have bought me; therefore I am yours,
and you can say what you like to me; but I warn you
that nothing you can say will interest me in the least.
I must marry you because fate has conspired against me,
and I do not see how I can avoid the hateful consum-
mation."

"Our courtship," said Mr. Moskins, "has been very
peculiar, and I daresay you consider me very eccentric ;
but your uncle kindly undertook to do all that was
necessary in the matter, for I am only a plain fellow—
good enough, I daresay, in my way, but, after all, only
a plain fellow. I've been in trade all my life, and I am
not ashamed of it. I have been tolerably successful, as
I daresay you have heard ; in fact," he added, with a
self-satisfied smile, "you will not be the wife of a pauper,
like the parson I have heard your uncle talk about."

Myra moved uneasily on her seat as he said this, and
exclaimed, in a firm but heart-broken voice, destitute of
that fire which used to animate her—

"I did not expect any delicacy from you, because your
breeding and education and mode of life have, of course,
kept you in ignorance of anything of the sort ; but perhaps you have had a mother, or a sister, or some female
relative, and I was foolish enough to think that you
might have imbibed some little feeling from them, or
that, in your intercourse with your fellow-tradesmen,
you might have picked up a little tact. Even a little
low cunning would be better than nothing."

Mr. Moskins looked perplexed at this speech, as if he did not understand it. His general idea of it, though, was shown by what he said directly afterwards.

" Well, we'll drop the curate, if you like. I didn't know, I'm sure, it was such a tender point. You ain't over and above complimentary to me, you know."

" I don't mean to be complimentary to you," she replied, boldly. " I tell you frankly, before I marry you, that you will espouse my person, but not my heart. That it is not in my power to give you ; and, even if it were, *you* should never have it. I marry you because it saves my uncle from something dreadful, and I consider it my duty to do so. I may be wrong, I am *sure* that I shall repent it ; but to consider it my duty is enough for me. I have no respect, no esteem, no regard for you, Mr. Moskins ; and I tell you so, frankly. Now, if you like to release me from my engagement, you can."

" Never !" he cried, emphatically. " I have bought you with my hard-earned gold, and I will teach you to love me afterwards. The first step is to make you mine. That is nearly accomplished. The rest will follow afterwards."

" You take me for what you know me to be," said Myra, in despairing accents ; " a woman without a heart."

Mr. Moskins made no reply for a moment, and then he said—

" I think you are very beautiful, and I take you for your beauty. Will that please you ?"

And he attempted to raise her hand to his lips and kiss it ; but she dashed it away from him with a frowning gesture, saying—

" You have not yet acquired the right to do that."

She swept out of the room a little proudly, as if pleased with the slight triumph she had gained.

CHAPTER XII.

"No, no, no! I will Die, but I cannot Marry that Man."

When Myra reappeared she was gaily decked. There was a wreath upon her brow, and orange blossoms never graced a lovelier victim. Her veil encircled her, and she was led into the carriage which awaited her. As she was driven along she wondered what church they were taking her to. Mr. Pompuss was to give the bride away, and he and his wife and Myra went together in one carriage; whilst Mr. Moskins and his best man, who happened to be his foreman, followed in another.

"What church are we going to?" demanded Myra.

"To Highgate Church," replied her uncle. "You see, the whole thing has been done in such a hurry that we are obliged to go to the nearest. We have just had time to get the licence, and give them a very brief notice; and that's all—and that's all, my dear."

Highgate Church! What memories those two words called up! It was there that she had first listened to the earnest tones of Frank Ogilvie—there that she had imbibed that reverence for all holy things which was her main characteristic. To such an extent did she carry her religious proclivities, that we have seen she did not hesitate to sacrifice her love to what she considered her duty, and to marry Mr. Moskins before a man whom she knew to be a perfect gentleman and a man of honour, and whom she felt loved her to distraction.

Such are the peculiarities and contradictions of feminine nature.

During the short drive Myra prayed that she might hear or see or meet nothing that could remind her of Frank Ogilvie. At such a time she could not bear it; it would be too much for her already over·wrought nerves. She was going to give up her independence, to give up everything she held dear, and her only hope of happiness in this world. She was very quiet and silent, and subdued.

Mr. and Mrs. Pompuss were in very good spirits. The former, because his plan had succeeded so well; and the latter, because the prophetic Doctor had predicted a universal catastrophe in a couple of months, and she was rejoicing that her daughter's marriage had taken place before the great destruction happened.

Mr. Moskins met his bride at the altar, and the little party waited for the coming of the priest. At last the little vestry-door opened, and a young man—very thin, very pale, but very handsome—walked into the church. His eyes were lustrous. Who shall say that they were not tinged with red? With his eyes cast upon the ground, he passed through the group, and pushing aside the gate in the centre of the rails which divided that part of the church where the Communion is usually read from the other, stood before them, to unite the man with the woman until death did them part. He seemed to be much occupied with his own thoughts, for he did not look up until he had opened the book, and then he fairly started a foot back; the book fell from his hands, and his whole body trembled convulsively.

"Is that the rector?" demanded Mr. Moskins of the beadle.

"He be the curate, Sir; and a nice young man too, which he is generally beloved by the 'ole parish, Sir,

and which they're beant a gentlemanlier young man
in the entire establishment of the Church of Hingland,
Sir," replied the beadle, in a tone of voice loud enough
to be heard by the person he was eulogizing. Gratitude
is always a sense of favours to come.

But the curate heard him not ; he stood with his eyes
staring, and his lips parted. A moment or so, however,
recalled him to himself, and he picked up the Church
Service which had dropped from his hand. Myra had
witnessed the whole of this remarkable scene, but she
made no sign. She had recognized Frank Ogilvie as
soon or sooner than he had noticed her; but she
remained as immobile as a block of marble from
the quarries of Carrára. She was rigid and stony.

Ogilvie, in a voice tremulous from agitation, began
to read the marriage ceremony. All was as still as
night ; Myra's heavy breathing was alone heard.
Ogilvie's voice was thick and husky. It was, in truth,
a terrible ordeal for him to undergo ; but he bore it
like a martyr. His faith upheld him ; although his pure
and faithful heart was torn to pieces by the tem-
pestuous passion which swept through its chambers.
It was madness to him to think that he should be compelled to marry the only being he loved, or ever had
loved, or ever would love, to another ; and such another! He saw at a glance what the man was ; and, while
he commiserated Myra, he hated her. He thought it
would have been better and happier for her to have cast
her lot with him than to have sought wealth and
gilded misery with the man who was soon to call her
his own. His own ! Oh ! there was a mine of madness
in the very thought. "His! his! Oh! let the hour
be cursed rather," he thought.

Then his mind changed a little, and he said, "If she
were worthy of my love, she would not now be standing
where she is ; nor would she have sought to insult and
crush me by bringing him to this church, of all others."

While he thought in this way he was reading the service mechanically. He knew it almost by heart, and he only looked upon the missal so that he might not meet the gaze of the woman he loved. There and then he would have forgiven her all, if she had only spoken one word to him; he would have worshipped her. He would have kissed her feet—kissed the ground her feet were now pressing, and have thought himself blest in doing so. But it was not to be.

As the service proceeded Myra looked so white beneath her veil that you might have taken her flesh for driven snow. After a time she tottered a little, and she would have fallen had not Mr. Pompuss supported her. Her aunt attributed all this to the agitation naturally to be expected on such an occasion.

"Poor dear!" she muttered to herself, "she's just like me. Why, when I married Pompuss—there, you might have knocked me down with a straw."

It was not likely that Myra, with her exquisite sensibility, could make a confidant of her aunt; so that worthy disciple of a prophetic parson was totally unacquainted with the real state of her niece's heart. She, good lady, thought she was marrying the man of her choice. She was perfectly well aware of her antipathy to Sir Philip Deverill, and she considered that her dislike to him arose through her feeling a preference for Mr. Isaac Moskins.

"I don't mind the man at all," she observed, when her husband first mooted the matter to her; "besides, he has money; but 1 don't exactly like the idea of having a husband whose Christian name is Isaac. Ike or Ikey are the only diminutives, and—well, there, we will let the subject drop; but, if you had been called Isaac, why, I wouldn't have lived with you a month, Pompuss—no, not a month."

Whilst Mrs. Pompuss was indulging the reflections

we have alluded to, the set phrases were being repeated which were to make Myra Fontaine and the tea dealer man and wife, to live together until death stepped in to separate them. Myra ground her teeth together in her agony; she felt the strongest inclination to turn round and tear the bridal finery from her, and, throwing it to the winds, rush from the precincts of the sacred edifice; but something—she knew not what—constrained her to stay where she was. Was it a hope of some intervention, on the part of Providence, to save her from her doom? An evangel at the last!

When Frank Ogilvie came to the words, "Wilt thou take this man to be thy wedded husband?" he looked up, and gazed at her. His eye caught hers. If ever there was such a thing as animal magnetism, or odic force, it was called into existence on that occasion. His looked thrilled through Myra. She could not remove her eyes from his countenance. She made no reply. Every one looked at her, but she was more marbly than ever

Frank Ogilvie slowly repeated the question prescribed in the Rubric; but he did what the Rubric did not authorize him to do. He dwelt on the words, "this man," and turned his eyes compassionately upon Myra. For a moment she wavered; then a soft light seemed to suffuse her eyes. She was translated, as it were, and crying in a clear voice, "No, no, no! I will die, but I cannot marry that man," she fell heavily upon the tesselated pavement of the chancel; and for a time her misery was forgotten: its great weight had passed from her.

Mr. Moskins, without uttering a syllable, turned on his heel, and, with great heavy strides, left the church. When he was in the porch, he jammed his hat down on his head, and said, between his teeth, "To think that I should be made such a d——d fool of!" And then he got into his carriage, and was driven off.

Frank Ogilvie ran to the font, utterly forgetful of his sacerdotal character, and brought some of the baptismal water in his hands, which he threw in Myra's upturned countenance. And it came to pass that after a time she revived, and she was borne out of the church, leaning upon her uncle's arm. And everybody was silent and preoccupied except Frank Ogilvie: and he danced about the floor of the vestry, almost wild with joy, for there was yet hope for him.

After all, the beadle and the pew-opener met together to talk over the scandal; and a grand gossip they had.

"My '" said the pew-opener, "wasn't it funny?"

"And didn't she seem to take on?" said the beadle.

"Ah! There's more there than either you nor I knows on," replied the pew-opener, sententiously. And with this oracular sentence on her lips, she went into the world of Highgate to disseminate the news.

"The curiousest thing as ever was," she said: "let alone when them six bridesmaids fainted at one time, and Jakes' widow dropped down dead at his funeral."

But Myra was reprieved.

CHAPTER XIII.

COLONEL BOWERING AND HIS SON.

A MELANCHOLY party was that which returned from Highgate Church. Myra was in a comatose state, half conscious, half unconscious, almost semi-animate. Mr. Pompuss was terribly alarmed at first, but he consoled himself with the idea that he had the money which Mr. Moskins had paid him as the price of his niece's hand; and that, he declared, no power on earth should wrest from him.

"He cannot prosecute me," thought the stockbroker. "I have done nothing illegal. It is a breach of contract, certainly, but not one for which I can be held responsible. I have done my part, and if the girl chooses at the last to kick over the traces, why, Moskins can't blame me. It's Moskins' luck, Sir—it's his luck."

"Yes, and infernal bad luck, too," Mr. Moskins would have replied, had the remark been addressed to him.

Mrs. Pompuss could only sigh, and exclaim—

"That passage in the Revelation of St. John is exactly applicable to this case. It is quite a coincidence."

"Bother the Revelation of St. John!" replied Mr. Pompuss, surlily.

When the carriage arrived Myra was sufficiently recovered to walk into the house without assistance.

"Come into the drawing-room, child, and have a glass of sherry, or something to put some life in you," said Mrs. Pompuss to her niece. "I declare, you look like a ghost."

Myra made no objection, and followed her aunt. What was her surprise, on entering the room, to perceive two gentlemen, who rose as they made their appearance. One was a man about sixty—tall, slight, and grey; the other, young, fair, and inclined to be stout.

Mrs. Pompuss stood still, as if the gentlemen were perfect strangers to her, when the elder of them exclaimed—

" My dear Mrs. Pompuss, is it possible you can have forgotten me ?"

" Whom have I the pleasure ——" began Mrs. Pompuss.

" Why, bless me !" cried her husband, coming in at the door, " it's Bowering ! Don't you remember, Liza ? Your memory can't be so bad as all that, eh ? —can't be so bad as all that ?"

Mrs. Pompuss opened her eyes, and replied—

" Dear me, John ! So it is. I remember Lieutenant Bowering well."

" Colonel now, my dear madam ; full Colonel," said her visitor, gaily. " Got my steps since I left England; thank God and the War-office."

" Oh, Colonel ! For shame ! That is just like you," simpered Mrs. Pompuss.

When Myra saw the strange people, she ran away and locked herself in her room, when she tore off her dress and bridal trappings, and then threw herself upon her bed, and wept bitterly—very bitterly. The tears of those who are young and unused to battle with the world are sometimes as bitter as the waters of Marah.

The Colonel, without noticing Mrs. Pompuss's remark, went on in a chatty sort of way, " As your husband and yourself were my dearest friends before I left England, and as you have often in your letters invited me to make your house my home for a week or so, when I

came back to the old country, if ever I did so, I have
not scrupled to avail myself of your invitation. This
young man is my son. You remember him, I daresay
—a young cub, when he went to Sandhurst. Well,
Ma'am, he got his commission by hard work, and now
he's a Captain ; was in one of the N.I. regiments, but
couldn't stand the niggers ; so exchanged into the 60th
Rifles. Been out now six years ; so I thought it wouldn't
do him any harm to exchange and come home a bit.
Nothing like England, after all, Ma'am—nothing. And
Billy—his name's Billy, you know—is mad after home."

Mr. Pompuss shook hands with the Colonel very
heartily, and said—

"I am delighted that you have come to see me,
Bowering. It shows you haven't forgotten ' Old lang
syne.' But where is Ada, Mrs. Bowering ?"

"That's the only cloud I've had," replied the Colonel.

"Why, you don't mean—eh ?"

"Truth, Sir, truth. Died on the voyage out."

And the Colonel looked pained and sad at the mournful reminiscence.

"Very sorry to hear that—very sorry indeed to hear
that," said Mr. Pompuss. Then he added, "Now, you
make this house your home, Bowering, as long as you
like to stay ; you Billy, too. You see, I know your name,
young gentleman. You must excuse me for the present.
I have to go into the City on particular business.
Urgent—very urgent. The Missis will do the honours.
We used to call her the Missis in Charterhouse-square—
eh, Colonel ?"

Colonel Bowering laughed, and showed a set of teeth
in excellent preservation, in spite of chutney and curry
powder.

"A word in your ear, Bowering," continued Mr.
Pompuss.

The Colonel drew near, and the broker said—

" Rather an unpleasant occurrence happened here, this morning. Myra ——"

"Fontaine's daughter?"

"Yes; quite a child when you left. Well, she was to have been married this morning; but when we got to the altar, and through the best part of the marriage service, she threw the man over, and swore that she would rather die than marry him, Sir—rather die than marry him. Reg'lar Crœsus, too—reg'lar Crœsus. Tell you more, after a bit, when I come back. Must be off now, though—must be off."

And Mr. Pompuss bustled out of the room, and went into the City.

Mrs. Pompuss went away to give orders about the rooms the two men were to occupy, and the Colonel and his son were left alone for a brief space, with the decanter before them. The Captain helped himself to some sherry in a tumbler, which his father observing, said—

" Won't do, Billy, my boy. You drink too much. It isn't brandy pawnee, you know."

"Oh! I know what I'm about," replied Billy. "These are your City friends, are they? Can't say I think much of them."

" My boy," said the Colonel, turning half round in his chair, and looking severely at him, " my boy, did you ever stop at an hotel?"

" Well, I have done such a thing."

"Oh! you have? Then, I suppose, you had the pleasure of paying the bill afterwards?" said the Colonel.

" I'd rather pay a bill than be a sponge," returned Captain Billy Bowering, doggedly.

" You can do as you like," said his father, pleasantly. "I don't want you. Go as soon as you like—go; now, if it suits you. I shall stop here. I haven't got the Mines of Golconda in my waistcoat-pocket. Wish to God I had."   G

To judge from his subsequent movements, it did not appear to suit the Captain to move from his present quarters, for he did not offer to move from where he was sitting.

"What was that girl in the veil? Private theatricals, I suppose?" he observed, after a pause.

"Private theatricals!" echoed his father. "Don't be a fool. Wasn't anything of the sort."

"Wasn't! Well, how did I know?"

"Fact is, they had a wedding, or were to have had, this morning, but the girl didn't like the man they'd got for her, and wouldn't have him; told him so, Sir, at the altar. I like her spirit. Just like her father."

"Who is she?"

"Why, Fontaine's daughter. You've heard me talk of Fontaine, haven't you? As nice a fellow as ever breathed."

"Wanted her to have some City cad, I suppose—eh?" said the Captain; "and she was too good a judge?"

"Don't you talk so loud, my boy. I've known walls listen, and talk, too," replied the Colonel.

"They may talk themselves into fits," said his son, "for what I care."

"I think I heard that Fontaine left some money," remarked Colonel Bowering, musingly. "In that case, there's a chance for you, Billy."

"For me? No, thank you. I'm not fond of your City Misses. Won't do for me, governor; so I tell you," answered the Captain, stroking his moustache.

At this juncture the servant entered, to conduct them to their rooms; and the Colonel and his son were duly installed as inmates of the broker's house at Highgate.

"I'm glad they've come," said Mrs. Pompuss. "They may help to cheer Myra up a bit, for she's dreadfully down-hearted, poor thing! It's quite shocking to see her."

CHAPTER XIV.

Mr. Moskins undertakes a Secret Mission.

ALTHOUGH Colonel Bowering's son was rather a rough sort of diamond, and what Mrs. Pompuss called vulgar, he was extremely amusing. His *forte* was giving recitations, and he was good-natured enough to extemporize to any extent whenever he was called upon.

A few evenings after the arrival of his father and himself, he displayed his singular powers, making even miserable Myra laugh. He could ventrilcquize, too, and sing a comic song. Getting on a chair, he turned up his coat-collar, brushed his hat the wrong way, screwed his mouth on one side, and, imitating a wheezy costermonger, gave them some anecdotes of the Lower Ten Thousand, beginning as follows:—

"We're awfully low down my way. We've been getting lower ever since Parliament refused to repeal the malt-tax; in fact, if we go on getting much lower, we shall leave the garrets and live altogether in the cellars. I like to be low. My ancestors for generations have been shamefully low. I had a uncle a area sneak, and a grandmother on my father's side who used to sell fish in Billingsgate. She was the identical fish-fag to whom Theodore Hook applied the distinguishing epithet of 'isosceles parallelogram,' which she thought was something new in the shell-fish line. My father was a man who worked under Government at Portland Island; and it was at Pentonville that I learnt to write, while my dutiful offspring, aged five, was a-roaring hisself

G 2

hoarse, singing 'Father, dear father, come 'ome,' which
he would have done with pleasure, only he laboured
under a slight disability. When I returned to the
bosom of my family I found my lad at a ragged-school,
and I took him away because Lord Shaftesbury was the
president, and once patted him on the head, regardless
of consequences. I can't bear the haristocracy; they're
so 'aughty. I belong to a trades' union, chiefly to do
the rattening and shootin' business, but I think of leaving; our secretary and I can't hit it. He says there
was a very good peer lost when he was born a brick-
layer. I shall withdraw my name from that union.
The secretary is too haristocratic for me. Perhaps my
services will be appreciated at Sheffield. I shall take
my wife, if I go there. She's good at blowing up, and I
can do the blasting. I'm so low, you know. There's a
bit of a sing-song down my way, and there's a nigger
who hits off a king fine. I had a talk with him one
night over a pot of 'arf-and-'arf, which he stood.
'Kings ain't of no account,' he says. 'No,' says I. 'It
was only yesterday I refused a glass of beer because the
public was called the King's Head.' 'Ah!' says he,
'that's what I wouldn't mind having a chop at.' And
then we went to a Conservative meeting at St. James's
Hall, and raised the Cap of Liberty on the platform.
We're so awfully low. Every one knows Betsey Baker;
at least, every one has heard of her. She is a lineal
descendant of Dick Turpin. It was she who fought the
beadle of St. Bride's in Fetter-lane, and got a black eye
and six months. It was Betsey who couldn't a-bear the
children of her sixth husband, and put the eldest on the
fire. Betsey was starred out in the papers when she bit
another woman's nose off in Spitalfields, and was afterwards tarred with oakum-picking. I'm in the tripe and
cat's-meat line now. I met Betsey the other day. She
had a pal with her, and we went into a public to have

a drop, and tossed who should pay. It was Betsey, and she said I was the hod man out, alluding to my having been in the bricklaying line. Betsey's friend was considerable put out at me not paying, and said, quite indignant, 'You've queer ways in these parts. When I lived at Acton, a man never let a woman pay.' 'Ah!' says I, winking at Bet, 'we don't act on that principle down here; and if you don't like it, you may take it out in cat's-meat;' which she did, going to the barrow, which was handy, and throwin' ha'porths like lightnin', and never leaving off till she'd shied half a boiled horse at me. Lor! 'ow the cats came thronging up! Three busted themselves on the spot, and two was carried to the nearest ospital in the agonies of internal conwulsions. I was standing by, looking quite pitiful, and wiping the corner of my eye with my shirt-tail, which I had extracted through a convenient aperture for that purpose, when Bet said, 'That's nothing, that ain't. She's so playful, the dear creature; you shouldn't say nothing to rile her.' If that was nothing, I wondered what something was with the dear creature! It's a strong-minded woman's boast that a husband shouldn't call his soul his own. If Mr. Samkins—that's the 'dear creature's' husband—ain't that man, I never see one. Call his soul his own! He wouldn't think of asserting ownership in a hair of his head. If he did, Mrs. S. would show him the blooming error he was committing. One more anecdote of Mrs. Samkins, and I have done. That lady's fondness for ancient Thomas is proverbial in the lower circles in which she moves. She does her half-quarterns regular. I was a-serving her with a ha'porth of the usual for her feline companion, when she drops the skewer and runs into the court, as if she couldn't help herself. It was a big boy a-'itting of hern. When she'd boxed him pretty nigh silly, she left off, and the boy's mother came. It was a sight then. Did you ever see two cats a-fighting on the tiles? In half-an-hour Mrs. Samkins left her opponent for dead; ten minutes afterwards she was eating winkles with a pin, and rocking the baby to the tune of—

    'Oh! so gently o'er me stealing,
      Came a wave of thought so sweet,—
    How we fought, and how I whopped her,
      Till she owned that she was beat.'"

When this was finished he changed his voice to that of a middle-aged lady, with a slight cold, and said—

"I am Mrs. Marshall, and I will tell you what I say when I call on my dear friend, Mrs. Sanderson."

Every one listened, and he commenced:—

"Ah! my dear Mrs. Sanderson, how delightful it is to see you so industrious! You work so hard that you deserve a statue. How pricked about your fingers are, though! Will not that be rather disagreeable when your gloves are off? But tell me, dear, how you like this neighbourhood? Very new? Why, yes, it is; but, of course, it is cheap; and, as I said to Marshall only last night, 'Of course, it is very suitable for people in their position.' How does your husband treat you since you have moved? Rather later in coming home, of course? It is some distance from the City and Kensington, isn't it? Culthorpe-street, is it? Marshall says he saw Sanderson talking to a little *party* in Cheapside, as he was coming home, a few days back. Perhaps he was telling her the time, or the way, or something. I shouldn't take any notice of it if I were you, dear. But, there, it is no use talking. Men will be men, all the world over; and I'm sure, I don't care what Marshall does if I don't know it, and so long as he gives me the money I ask for. What an angel you must be, dear! Why? Because you are *so* good. I could no more sit at home in that old brown Holland wrapper, and mend the children's frocks, than I could fly. Someone must do it? To be sure ; but, depend upon it, the more a woman puts up with the more she may. Oh, but I must tell you ; it had nearly slipped my memory. You know that Mrs. Somerville Wormwood? Well, she saw you at church last Sunday with the new Japanese silk you showed me. ' Oh,' she said to someone who repeated her remarks to me, ' of course, Sanderson could not afford to give her that. He has enough to do to keep a house over his head, and dress himself, on his three hundred a-year. It must be a present. They do say that she had a great many admirers before her marriage, and ——.' There, don't get excited. ' Odious creature !' I said directly, ' I don't believe a word of it.' But when these reports get about, they are so difficult to contradict. Don't you think, dear, your eldest looks a little so-so under the eyes ? They tell me the measles are quite prevalent now, and—yes, the skin is a little rough. Is that a rash on the dear little fellow's face ? You hope not ? So do I. It is so dangerous for children to get ill. They are off in a moment. There was poor Mrs. Ledbury's first. Don't make you nervous ? Not for the world. I really thought you were more courageous. By the way, did you hear there had been several cases of cholera in Kensington ? What ! that was in the low parts ? Well, all I know is, the cholera is frightfully contagious ; and I should be off to Brighton if I heard of it within a mile of Belgravia. I really felt I was running quite a risk in coming to see you ; I did, indeed. The panic, they say, is worse than ever in the City. Do you think the bank which your husband is in is safe ? He says so ? Ah ! but he mayn't know. What a dreadful thing it would be if it were to break, and he were thrown out of employment ! What *would* you do ? I don't suppose your friends could afford to keep you, and Marshall says Sanderson's

couldn't. Very odd, people won't mind their own business? So it is, my dear That is just the remark I
made to Rosa Wright when she said you would never
do in your new house; for, what with the rent and the
taxes, and the gas and the servants, and the water and
the parties ;—what! you don't mean to give any? Oh!
that is a great mistake, and you will find it so. Your
friends will get tired of entertaining you if you show
them no return. You don't want to go out? Why,
my dear child, you might just as well be in a convent.
But I must run away. Good-bye, dear. Ta, ta! little
ones. I'm sure that boy's sickening for the measles.
Good-bye. Don't come to the door. I can let myself
out. I hope the bank won't break ; it would be so bad
for you. I'll come again soon."

In spite of the *fiasco* in the church, Mr. Moskins was
not to be deterred from visiting the Pompusses. Myra
always left the room when he entered, but he remained,
talking to Colonel Bowering, his son, and Mrs. Pompuss. The Colonel flattered him because he was rich.
They dined together, and no one could order such a
dinner as Colonel Bowering. Witness a *menu* at the
Globe :—

MENU.—Salmon en Mayonnaise, galantines de volaille,
roast chickens, aspic de foies gras de Strasbourg, roast
beef, hams, tongues, larded chickens, boiled chickens,
lobster salads, roast lamb, patés de volaille, wine jelly,
suédoise de fraises, punch jelly, Charlottes à la Bohé-
mienne, compotes de fruits, cremés Françaises, Charlotte
Russe, patisserie, truites.

Not a bad bill of fare for two men, as Mr. Moskins
admitted ; but the bill—that was awful! However,
men who make millions do not care about the expense
of entertainments

Colonel Bowering had travelled a great deal, and
when young he had been an *attaché* at the Court of

Bohemia. He quickly learnt all about Mr. Moskins' connection with the Grand Trunk Railway, and he conceived an idea which he did not lose much time in broaching.

The situation at the stockbroker's house remained unchanged. Myra would have nothing more to say to Mr. Moskins, in spite of her uncle and aunt's remoustrances. As the money left her, which her uncle had embezzled, was restored, Sir Philip Deverill could do nothing ; and he retired into private life, to indulge in the luxury of gnashing his teeth, and occasionally weeping.

Colonel Bowering and his son stayed as long as they could with propriety at Highgate, and then they took their leave and some lodgings in the immediate vicinity.

One day the Colonel purposely contrived to run up against Mr. Isaac Moskins, on the steps of the stockbroker's office.

" Ah, how d'ye do ?" he said. " Glad to see you."

" Good morning, Sir," replied Mr. Moskins, frigidly.

He was always stiff and formal in business.

" I have just dropped in to do an option," continued the gay and gallant Colonel. " I never do much ; only dabble occasionally. Not like you Leviathans; go and do your tens of thousands. I am satisfied with a mild century and a half per cent. For instance, I bought a hundred Bohemians to-day. Not that I expect to make much by them, but some day ——"

He hesitated, and looked knowingly at no one in particular.

Mr. Moskins regarded him as he would a dangerous lunatic.

" I should have thought," he said, "that Pompuss could have told you something about Grand Trunks."

" The opinion of a broker, Sir, isn't worth two-

pence," cried the Colonel, snapping his fingers derisively.
" I know ——"

Here he regarded the great man with an oracular
stare.

" What do you know ?" asked the great man, made
anxious in spite of himself.

" Will you dine with me to-day ?"

" Where ?"

" Never mind where. Will you dine with me ?" persisted the Colonel. "If you consent, you are my property,
and I can take you where I like."

" Well, I don't mind if I do.   I don't know that I
have anything to do; and I may as well eat my chop
with you as have a sixpenny plate of meat elsewhere."

The Colonel indulged in cacchination.

"How killing you great men are!" he said. " By Jove!
there is a wonderful amount of dry humour about you.
Fancy a man who is going to make millions before he
dies, talking about a sixpenny plate of meat !"

" When I first came to town ——" began Mr. Moskins.

" Ah, that's another thing altogether.   I don't suppose you were quite so well off *then*," interrupted the
Colonel, not thinking it politic to allow him to humiliate
himself by relating his antecedents, though he knew
very well he was a self-made man.

" I hate those self-made fellows," he once observed
to his son Billy; " they are always talking about the
office broom, and coming to London with only a shilling.
I think they are as bad as the men who go to India in
the Civil Service, make a little money, and come back
here as if they were demi-gods."

" So, you'll dine with me ?" he said.

" With pleasure."

" Meet me at Pompuss's at four o'clock, sharp."

" I will be there, Sir."

The Colonel raised his hat just a little bit and walked
away, while Moskins entered the stockbroker's office.

Since we last accompanied him into that sanctum a great change had come over the market. An organized gang of men had been operating for a fall in bank and railway shares, and with a marked success.

" What's in the wind ? Anything new ?" inquired Moskins, as he entered the office.

" Banks and railways, Sir ; nothing else. No speculation in anything else. Markets are very flat. Consols for the account ninety-four five-eighths. Money is at two per cent."

" No alteration in the Bank-rate ?"

" None whatever, Sir."

" Very bad. So they are Bearing banks—eh ?"

" To a frightful extent. There was quite a run on the Agha and Plasterman's yesterday."

" Ha ! ha !" laughed Isaac Moskins. " I've got considerably more than half a million there, Pompuss ; and I wouldn't mind doubling my account to-morrow ; it's as safe as the London and Westminster, or the Bank of England."

" I'm not so sure about that," replied Pompuss, shaking his head.

" I am. How are Trunks ?"

" Nowhere. A drug in the market."

Taking up the paper, Mr. Moskins sat down, and amused himself with gleaning the news and making abstruse and complicated calculations with the aid of a pen and half a sheet of note-paper.

When he found that the Bears were attacking a certain railway, he basely joined their ranks, and sent Pompuss into the market to sell fifty thousand of stock which he had not in his possession to deliver. But that fact never burdens the conscience of your Christian operator.

The Colonel kept his appointment, and drove his guest in a neatly-appointed mail phaeton which he had borrowed from a friend, to Cremorne.

"I ordered dinner by telegraph here," he said. "It being summer, I thought you would like to hear the music, see the dancing, and look at the women, you know."

Mr. Moskins said he did not at all object. He was passionately fond of music; and as to women, he rather liked looking at them.

They had what the Colonel called a "very decent dinner;" and afterwards they smoked some Havannahs, which the Colonel carried in his own case, and pronounced to be very choice. The sparkling wine was good, so they stuck to that in preference to the logwood, as Bowering called the port.

"Now, my dear Sir, I am going to talk unreservedly to you," he said, leaning over the table, and fixing his eye on his guest; "because I think I see my way to making a lot of money, and you are the man to help me to it."

"I'm always open to embark in a good thing," replied Moskins. "But first of all, mind you, I must satisfy myself that it is a good thing; and there are few better judges of what's what than your humble servant."

"That I believe," said the Colonel, emphatically.

"Now, what's your plan?"

"It has reference to those Bohemian Railways."

"Ha! ha! ha!" roared Mr. Moskins.

He was laughing him to scorn.

"My dear, Sir, listen before —— "

"I've no faith in them; so I tell you, once for all."

"But —— "

"Once bit, twice shy, my good fellow," replied Isaac Moskins.

"That proverbial philosophy," said the Colonel, with dignity, "is all very well in the nursery. Common sense, however, and patience have before now triumphed

over many obstacles. If you will have the kindness
to listen to what I am going to say, you will be more
in a position to answer me, and pronounce an opinion
upon my scheme."

"I beg your pardon," said Moskins ; "but Grand
Trunks are *such* a swindle, and have been so shamefully exposed, that —— "

"Never mind. I was once an *attaché* at the Court
of Bohemia. All you want is a concession."

" I know that. But a concession is precisely what
we can't get."

" I can put you in the way of getting it," said the
Colonel, pausing to see what effect this shot would
have upon his listener.

Mr. Moskins opened his eyes very wide indeed.
All the merriment vanished from his face. He was
as staid and sober as a judge now.

" I take you," he answered. " A thousand pardons
for my stupidity in not understanding you at first.
Your plan, of course, is for us to buy up all the stock
in the market, and then go over to Bohemia, and
obtain the concession which will rehabilitate the stock
in public favour."

" That is it to an iota."

" It's a great plan, by George, Sir—it's a great plan !
You have propounded it to me because I have the
money requisite for carrying the thing through ?"

" Exactly."

" It'll do, Sir. I can see at a glance that the thing's
feasible. We shall make millions. How do you propose to proceed ?"

" We shall have to bribe right and left, for the
country is in a most corrupt state."

" Never mind that. I never refuse to throw out
a sprat to catch a herring."

" This is the slack time of the year. Every one is

travelling, or going to travel; so that our absence will not give rise to suspicion."

" I have six different brokers," said Mr. Moskins. "All of them shall be at once employed in buying up Grand Trunks, and in a week from to-day I shall have made all my preparations, and be quite ready to accompany you."

" That is agreed, then," said the Colonel, hardly able to conceal his joy.

After some more conversation, they left the gardens, mutually pleased with one another.

Colonel Bowering's plan was to go to Bohemia, and gain access to the powers that could assist them in their enterprise, which he, from his former position there, could easily do. If they could obtain a concession from the king to construct the railway, operations could commence, and the stock would take a sudden jump upwards of ten or twenty per cent. If Moskins held all the stock, of course he would reap the major portion of the profit, for he would have the market in his own hands, and might sway it one way or the other, as he pleased.

At the time appointed Mr. Moskins and Colonel Bowering started for Bohemia.

CHAPTER XV

Mr. Moskins makes Millions, and Frank Ogilvie goes Abroad.

One fine morning a paragraph appeared in the daily journals, under the heading of "Latest Foreign News" (through Mr. Reuter's agency), to the following effect :—

"The King of Bohemia has granted a concession to an English company for the construction of a Grand Trunk Railway through the entire length of his Majesty's kingdom, and he has further agreed to subsidize the company to the extent of one-half of its paid-up capital; repayment of this advance to be guaranteed out of the first twenty years' receipts, and to be further secured on the line itself, its rolling stock, plant, &c."

When Pompuss read this, he was nearly mad with disappointment.

"Good God!" he said, as he felt like tearing his hair, "this will send Bohemians up to ten premium. There will be a rise of ten or fifteen per cent. this very day, and I haven't a solitary ha'porth of scrip!"

Rushing madly into the "house," he endeavoured to buy, but there were at least a hundred brokers besieging the jobbers, and all animated with the same intention.

Bohemian Grand Trunks were certainly in demand. The jobbers found, on consultation, there was positively no stock in the market, and they grew alarmed.

They had sold what they did not possess, and as they began to hold back, the outside public thought they were waiting for better prices, and the demand became so fast and furious, that Grand Trunks at one o'clock were quoted ten premium, whereas the night before they had been five and twenty dis.

A little before one, Mr. Vokins, a great broker, received a telegram from Paris to this purport :—

"Mr. Isaac Moskins, Paris, to Mr. Vokins, Throgmorton-street, London.—Telegraph immediately the price of Grand Trunks."

Shortly after one, Mr. Vokins telegraphed to his principal :—

"Unprecedented rise. Grand Trunks, ten premium, and rapidly going up."

At half-past one, Mr. Vokins received the following message :—

"Sell a hundred thousand, and deliver the scrip, and telegraph prices."

At a quarter past two Mr. Moskins, who had never left the Paris Telegraph-office, received this message from his broker :—

"Have realized. Prices still going up."

To which Mr. Moskins replied—

"Sell another hundred thousand."

This was done, and the rapacity of the buyers a little appeased. Grand Trunks closed at eleven premium.

The next day Mr. Moskins arrived in London. Colonel Bowering had stayed in Bohemia to look after the interests of the Company. He had done this at Mr. Moskins' especial request.

Moskins had travelled night and day to reach London, and he proceeded to the City without changing his shirt or staying to be shaved. He arrived at the office of Mr. Pompuss before the " house " opened. Pompuss received him with open arms.

"I am so glad you have arrived," he exclaimed. "Grand Trunks are going up like smoke. There is no mistake about it. They are the things to buy!"

"To sell, you mean," said Mr. Moskins, correcting him, with a smile.

"If you hold largely."

"I do. How many did you buy for me?"

"Something enormous."

"Well, go into the market, and sell every scrap."

Mr. Pompuss looked at his client in a deprecatory manner; but he knew him too well to refuse to execute the order on the ground of inexpediency. So he went and did as he was told.

Moskins went from one broker to another, and sold his stock while the fever for buying was at its height.

Before leaving London he had bought up all the stock of the Bohemian Grand Trunk Railway. He now reaped the benefit of his sagacity.

Without the least exaggeration, he had, in less than two months, made millions.

Putting his profits on this one transaction side by side with what he had made before, his balance at Agha and Plasterman's a little exceeded three millions of money.

If he had been a great man before, what was he now?

He gave up his shop, and took a very big house in a very fashionable part of London. But, although he might have successfully wooed a peeress, he remained true to his first love, and made fresh advances to Pompuss for the hand of his niece.

The stockbroker was willing enough that he should have the girl; but, if it is true that you can bring a horse to the water and yet not make him drink, it was true, in her case, that you can take a girl to the church and yet not succeed in making her wed.

H

The world did not treat Pompuss well. His little speculations did not answer. Things went wrong with him, and he borrowed first one-half, then the other, of his niece's fortune, and it went the way of the other money he had lost.

It became doubly—trebly important to him that Myra should make a good match, and he implored her to have Mr. Isaac Moskins; but she steadily refused.

Affairs were in this condition when Colonel Bowering came back from Bohemia.

His first visit was, of course, to the millionaire, whom he found in his big house in the fashionable part of London.

Mr. Moskins received him coldly, not exhibiting a tithe of the amiability and friendship he had professed for him when the negotiations were going on, for it was admitted then that the Colonel was mainly instrumental in enabling the City tradesman to make millions.

Moskins knew very well that Bowering had come for his share of the spoil, and he had determined to give him as little as possible.

The Colonel had foolishly relied on Moskins' honour, and had not bought any stock before leaving England ; so that he was completely in his power, more especially as no agreement existed between them.

He did not anticipate any difficulty, however. " The man has made heaps of money," he said to himself ; " and he cannot object to part with a couple of hundred thousand, which will amply satisfy me, and make me comfortable for the remainder of my pilgrimage in this sublunary sphere."

He was mistaken in his estimate of Mr. Moskins' character, as he soon found out.

" I have arranged everything out there," said the Colonel, throwing himself into a chair, and lighting a cigar, when he had exchanged greetings with his co-adjutor.

By "out there" he meant, of course, Bohemia.

"Oh !" said Moskins, also lighting a cigar.

"I think," continued Bowering, "that you must admit that I put you up to a good thing, and assisted you pretty well to carry it out."

"Not such a very good thing, after all."

"Eh ?"

"Nothing to howl at," said Mr. Moskins.

"I don't want you to howl at anything; but you have made a lot of money," replied the Colonel, over whose face there came a shade of displeasure.

"Who says so ?"

"People generally."

"What do they say ?"

"That you are the man who made millions."

"Of what ?"

"Pounds, of course."

Mr. Moskins laughed discordantly.

"I thought you were old enough not to believe all you hear, Colonel," he exclaimed. "Why, my good Sir, if they said I had made thousands over this Bohemian spec., they would be nearer the mark."

"Thousands !"

"Yes, a few ; say a hundred altogether ; and I'll act fairly with you. You shall have half. The half of one hundred—fifty, isn't it ? Well, I'll give you a cheque on my bankers, Agha and Plasterman s, for that sum. Come now, you can't say I'm not treating you handsomely.

Forced to restrain his resentment, which well-nigh choked him, for fear he should lose even that modicum, the Colonel gulped down his anger, and took the cheque. When he had it safely in his pocket, he exclaimed—

"You d——d old scoundrel ! I consider that you

have shamefully robbed me, and given me something less than a half per cent. on your winnings. Clever as you think yourself, you may find that you are too sharp by half; for, by G—! I will never rest until I've ruined you."

Mr. Moskins smiled, and the Colonel, slamming the door, left the room in a rage.

About that time, Frank Ogilvie, the poor curate, sought an interview with Myra, which she accorded him.

He was about to leave the country, but he could not go until he had seen and wished her good-bye.

Some influential patron had offered him a bishopric among some blacks inclined to cannibalism, and he had accepted it. It was a barren honour. The country was very deadly to Europeans; but he went. His friends said he was tired of his life, and perhaps they were not far wrong. However, if that were the case, he wished to die in the service of his Lord and Master.

He called at the stockbroker's house in Highgate, and found that he was not to be admitted. The servant, evidently obeying instructions he had received from his employers, declared that Miss Fontaine was staying with some friends in the country.

The curate bowed his head meekly, and went away.

For days he contrived to walk past the house, and frequented the place where he thought there would be a chance of meeting with her, but without success.

If the truth must be told, Mr. Ogilvie had a leaning to what is called the High Church party. He was a Ritualist, and very much in favour of clerical vestments. At his church, named All Saints', he had established a mild form of Confessional. That is to say, any young lady, or, for the matter of that, any poor mendicant sinner who wished to confess a sin or any number of sins, had only to come to the church in the morning between the hours of eight and ten, when Mr. Ogilvie would receive them in the sacristy, and, though he did not venture to absolve them in true Roman fashion, he would listen to the pitiful stories told him, and give his advice in quite a paternal or fraternal manner, as the case might be; and this with the full permission and cognizance of his superior, the rector.

It came to Myra's ears that Frank Ogilvie had been made a bishop, and, these things do travel so quickly, that he was going to leave the country. Thinking it odd that he did not come to see her, she made up her mind that she would see him. After what had passed, she did not think she could visit him as she had done on a former occasion, with any propriety. So, having a few tiny sins on her conscience, she determined to go to All Saints' in the morning and confess them. Accordingly, she studied a little book, called "'The Path to Confession made Straight,' by a Layman," which Frank Ogilvie had written at Exeter College, Oxford, before he took orders, and which was very High Church indeed in its tenor and contents. If this " Path " had been followed in all its entirety, it would assuredly have led its admirers to Rome; but if Archbishop Manning is to be believed, this is nothing remarkable now-a-days, as all the rank and talent of the country lean towards the Apostolic See.

The " Path " distinctly ordered its readers to fast before visiting the sacristy. So Myra started without her breakfast, looking very interesting in a black silk dress, a velvet jacket, the smallest of small bonnets without strings; round her neck a string of beads, from which was pendant a long ebony cross. She had not arrived at a crucifix as yet. Her gloves were lavender colour, and fitted her to perfection. In her hand she carried a Common Prayer-book and the "Path to Confession."

It is difficult to say whether any animal magnetism

had informed Frank Ogilvie of the visit his lady-love was going to pay him, but he was very uneasy and restless. He had sat half-an-hour in the sacristy without receiving any penitent, and was thinking that his morning would be an unprofitable one, when the verger opened the door, and admitted a veiled lady.

Frank started. He recognized that statuesque form in a moment, but she had sought him in his capacity of a priest, and not as a friendly acquaintance ; therefore he subdued his feelings, and, standing up, motioned her to a *prie-Dieu*, which stood in the centre of the sacristy, a plain, circular, whitewashed apartment, paved with encaustic tiles.

The beautiful penitent walked to the kneeling-stool and deposited her book upon the floor, then clasping her hands together. Before her was a table, upon which burned two large candles. In the centre of the table was a bronze crucifix. The table was covered with a heavy, pall-like, velvet cloth, which hung over the sides, touching the ground. On this was embroidered in letters of gold I.H.S. The sacristy was lighted by means of a skylight, which had been filled with stained glass, admitting only a dim, religious light, which made the scene all the more impressive.

Taking a common rush-bottomed chair, Frank Ogilvie drew it to the left side of Myra, and sat down, repeating a prayer in Latin. When that was finished he exclaimed—

"If you have come to unburden your mind to me in my ministerial capacity, do so, and I will comfort you according to my ability."

Then Myra, casting down her eyes and looking very lovely in her penitential confusion, replied—

"I am very miserable, because I am compelled to disobey the guardian chosen for me by my father, who wishes me to marry a man whom I do not love. What am I to do? Is a guardian justified in compelling a child to sacrifice her future happiness in obedience to his will?"

Wonderfully impassive was the young clergyman's face, as he replied—

"There is no limit to filial obedience."

"No limit?" repeated Myra.

"None."

"You give me no hope. You bid me go home and obey, in defiance of my feelings?"

"Return, and deck yourself for the sacrifice," said Ogilvie, in a sepulchral voice. "The fifth commandment is the only one with promise, and your days shall not be long in the land if you do not honour your father and your mother. Your guardian stands in *loco parentis*—that is, in the place of a father to you; and to disobey him would, in my humble judgment, be a deadly sin."

"And this thing must be done even if I die in the doing of it?" asked Myra.

"Yes; the thing must be done, even if you die in the doing of it," answered Ogilvie.

He seemed perfectly unmoved. No stoic could have been more indifferent than he was.

There was a pause, during which nothing was heard but the plashing of Myra's big scalding tears upon the ornamental floor.

"Have you aught else to be advised upon?" he asked.

Myra rose to her feet. She looked at him for a moment so entreatingly, but found no responsive glance in his eye. He was still the priest, and gave no indication of ever having been on friendly terms with the lovely girl before him.

Unable to contain herself any longer, she cried, in a loud, thrilling voice—

"Oh! Frank, Frank! Speak to me. I can bear it no longer. Speak to me, Frank. They tell me you are going away for years to a strange country, and I may never, never see you again."

And this man—made of iron, as he was—melted before the fire of her manner, and, speaking softly like a child, said—

"Yes, they have told you truly. I am going abroad because I cannot live here without you. Thousands of miles away, I may forget you."

"No, no. You will not forget me."

"I trust so. The Church shall be my bride. I will live a life which will fit me for the after-crown."

"Take me with you. Frank, Frank! I will sacrifice all for you!" cried the sobbing girl.

"You shall sacrifice nothing for me," he answered, slowly and deliberately. "My voyage and my mission would be accursed were I to rob a parent of his daughter. I should expect the avenging winds to sink the vessel in which I sailed, or the savages amongst whom I must dwell to kill me, ere I had been a week on their land. No, my sister—for as such I regard you—my dear sister in the Lord, we must part."

"Perhaps for ever."

"It is as One greater than I wills it."

"Oh, it is so dreadful to think that I may never see you again."

"Watch and pray. We may meet elsewhere," replied Ogilvie, raising his arm and pointing upwards.

Myra felt everything swimming before her eyes; she sank towards the ground; she remembered strong arms supporting her, and then all was a blank.

When she came to herself, the verger was supporting her in the sacristy. A cup of water stood by his side.

Frank was nowhere to be seen.

"Are you better, Miss?" asked the verger.

"Yes, thank you," she said, staring wildly around her ; "I am well and strong again now. It was but a passing faintness."

Raising and drawing her veil over her face, she picked up her books, and giving the man a half-sovereign, left the church.

In one week from that time Frank Ogilvie left England, setting sail for the antipodes.

CHAPTER XVI.

The Millionaire writes " M.P." after his Name.

Now that Isaac Moskins was doubly and trebly a millionaire, in the fullest acceptance of that grandiloquent term, he determined to become an M.P

Accordingly, when a vacancy occurred for the Borough of Lambeth, he came forward and issued an address. The walls were placarded with " Moskins for Lambeth," "Moskins and Purity of Election," when his agents were bribing right and left to insure his return ; "Moskins and Reform ;" "Vote for Moskins, the Man of the People."

Mr. Moskins' address was as follows :—

" To the Free and Independent Electors of Lambeth.

"Gentlemen,

"I beg most respectfully to offer myself as a candidate to represent you in the Commons House of Parliament.

"Many of you are already well acquainted with my political sentiments, but the time has now arrived when it is necessary that I should issue an explicit address to the whole constituency.

"I am in favour of carrying out Free-trade to the fullest extent, as advocated by that great and patriotic man, Richard Cobden.

"I am a firm supporter of religious liberty; and though a member of the Church of England, I would vote for its separation from the State, for throwing the Universities completely open to every denomination of religion, and against all future religious endowments by Government.

"I look upon the extension of education to the whole people as a necessity, believing it to be the great lever for elevating our population, and the chief means by which vice and crime are to be encountered.

"While we may congratulate ourselves on the character of the Reform Bill of 1867, still it has not done away with the necessity, in my opinion, for vote by ballot, to which I am sure we must yet resort, as the only feasible remedy against bribery, intimidation, and corrupt influences.

"I believe that there is room for considerable economy in our enormous national expenditure without impairing the efficiency of our defences, or endangering that security which ought ever to be maintained.

"I am opposed, as a rule, to all intervention in the affairs of other countries.

"I regard the improvement in the dwellings of the working classes, and everything which has a tendency to elevate them, as subjects of paramount importance.

"For the Metropolis, I am in favour of equalization of Poor-rates ; of obtaining a pure, ample, and cheap supply of Water and Gas ; and of securing for the public all possible open spaces.

"Ireland presents to Parliament great difficulties, in overcoming which firmness should be tempered by conciliation and kindness, with an earnest endeavour to make that fine country a contented and happy integral part of the United Kingdom.

"With regard to all matters affecting your local interests, I shall always be ready to confer with you and fully to perform my duty in relation to them.

"Being satisfied that the political sentiments of the

great majority of your Borough and those I entertain
are identical, should you do me the high honour of
returning me as your representative in Parliament,
I hope to prove that I am not unworthy of your confidence.

"I have the honour to be,

"Your most obedient Servant,

"ISAAC MOSKINS."

Amongst the most active canvassers against him was
Colonel Bowering, who, as if to show him that his
vengeance could be active as well as passive, took service under the banner of his adversary.

In spite of all efforts to the contrary, the power of
gold triumphed, and Mr. Moskins was returned to Parliament by a triumphant majority.

While the great man was flourishing, Mr. Pompuss
was getting worse and worse. A spell of evil seemed
to be cast over him. So unlucky was he, that he was
compelled to advertise his house and furniture at
Highgate to be sold by auction, intending to reside in
lodgings.

When Isaac Moskins saw the advertisement in the
papers, he smiled grimly. The house was to be sold
by a well-known auctioneer, at the Mart, in Token-
house-yard. Thither he went, and bought it at a stiff
price.

Ten minutes afterwards, Pompuss rushed in and exclaimed to the auctioneer—

"Is it all over?"

"Yes," was the reply.

"What did it fetch?"

"More than I expected, by some hundreds."

"Who is the purchaser?"

"Here's his card. It's that fellow who made so

much in Grand Trunks. Just got in for Lambeth.
Moskins his name is."

"Good God! what's he bought it for?" gasped the
stockbroker, not knowing whether this was to be good
or bad for him.

When he returned to his office, he was not in the
least surprised to see Isaac Moskins waiting for him.

A pleasant smile, such as the earth's lucky ones wear
upon their countenances, sat gracefully upon the millionaire's face.

"Glad to see you, Sir. Take a chair. Haven't had the
pleasure of doing any business for you for a long time."

"I have so many brokers," was the apologetic reply.
"But I flatter myself that I distribute my favours
equally. How's the wife?"

"Nicely, thank you."

"And your niece?"

"Poorly, very poorly; hasn't been herself this long
time. Wants change of air, I think; but things have
been going so cross with me, I can't afford them a
cheque, or they should have a month at Boulogne."

"No luck, eh?"

"Not a ha'porth, Sir. Everything I touch is sure
to get crabbed. There is some fatality about it; that
I verily believe."

"Anything new?"

"Only a fall in Agha and Plasterman's."

"What is the cause of that?"

"Selling Bears of it. It is an organized and deli-
berate attempt, Sir, to depreciate a valuable security;
and if the men could only be found, in my opinion
they have rendered themselves liable to be indicted for
conspiracy."

"It is nothing," said the man of money, carelessly.

"Perhaps not; but you must recollect that there has
been a steady drop for the last month, and that alarms
people at a distance. Country holders, for instance,

withdraw their balances, and the news goes abroad.
You have branches in India. Suppose there is a run
on all your branches; you must suspend payment ; you
can't help yourselves."

"I am not afraid. It is by giving in to this panic
sort of fear that banks are broken. Suppose I were to
withdraw my two or three millions; that would cripple
them, Sir, wouldn't it ?"

"Of course."

"Then I sha'n't do it, that's all."

A clerk came in with the one o'clock list of prices.
Moskins glanced over it.

"Anything I can do for you this morning?" asked
Pompuss, who was, alas! greatly shorn of his pomposity
now.

"I've a fancy for Turkish. Buy me a hundred
thousand Consolides for the account."

"Very well. I'll be back directly."

It soon got rumoured about that Moskins, who was
regarded as a wonderfully acute speculator, was a large
buyer of Consolides; and, before the "house" closed,
the stock went up a half per cent. The next day Moskins sold, and took the nimble ninepence.

When the stockbroker came back, Moskins said,
playfully, "I bought a house to-day, Pompuss."

"And I sold one. That is the difference between
us," mournfully replied Pompuss.

"Where are you going to live now ?"

"God knows. I suppose we shall get in somewhere,
as long as I can make money enough to keep a roof
over our heads. Heaven, they say, tempers the wind
to the shorn lamb."

"Does Myra ever speak of me ?"

"Sometimes."

"In a complimentary manner ?"

"Oh, yes," replied Pompuss, inventing a pleasant
fiction.

" Pompuss," said the millionaire, very gravely.

" Well," replied the stockbroker, moving uneasily.

" You're a liar, Pompuss! I don't mean to insult you, but I like plain English; it hits people so hard. It's all nonsense to talk about polished satire. There isn't one man in fifty who's got sense enough to see a carefully wrapped-up sarcasm; but you speak to him in terse Anglo-Saxon, which he can understand; it beats all your Norman-French, as I may say."

" I am not aware in what way I have deviated from the truth," answered Pompuss, very red in the face.

" You know that girl hates me as the devil hates holy water."

" I don't think her feeling is so strong as that."

" I don't think at all about it; I know it is. She's a fool for her pains; but I don't dislike her any the less for it. I want her, and I haven't given up all idea of winning her yet."

" You haven't ?" cried the stockbroker, joyfully.

He had given up all hopes of anything in that quarter.

" Bravo, my boy. That's the sort of spirit. Faint heart never won fair lady."

" There, that will do," said Moskins. " I hate so much d——— talk. I'll tell you what I'll do. I'll make a settlement on the girl, as I said before. I'll give you your house; and I'll do more than that. You shall have all my business, Pompuss. Think of that, my boy; all my business !"

Pompuss well knew that the commission arising from Moskins' business, which was very extensive, was of itself a small fortune.

" You're very kind," he said, while the tears sprang to his eyes at the prospect of damming up the river through which the tide of bad luck was flowing. " I don't deserve so much kindness."

"You fool!" said the Anglo-Saxon Moskins; "what are you snivelling at? I don't care two pins for you, and I don't know that I should pick you out of the gutter to-morrow, if I saw you lying there as I passed by. It's the girl I want. Care for you! Not you, you old Jackass!"

Mr. Pompuss, as this tirade fell upon his ears, stopped his tears, and dried his eyes with the sleeve of his coat.

"You old crocodile!" ejaculated Moskins.

"Really, Sir, this language—I can't; my self-respect won't allow ——"

"Don't make a Judy of yourself," interrupted the millionaire, scathing the lachrymose stockbroker with a look. "Come out, and have a bottle of sparkling, and talk the matter over. I want the girl. You know my terms. I'll give you a month to manage things in; and if you can't do it in that time, why, as the house and furniture is mine, I'll sell you up—I will, by G——! So, don't you go and make any blooming error about it, my boy."

Although Pompuss was not very refined, he could not help feeling shocked at the utter vulgarity of the millionaire.

"If it were not for his money and my desperate circumstances," he muttered, " I'd rather see the girl in her grave than his wife. I don't know whether it wouldn't be better as it is; but poverty is such a bitter pill to swallow. You can make yourself tolerably comfortable so long as you have money, but once be without it, and hell itself is preferable to the life you lead in this country."

He went with Moskins to a tavern in the neighbourhood, where they sat down and had a salmon cutlet, after which they indulged in a bottle of Moselle. Over the wine, Moskins opened his heart to Pompuss, and told him he could not live without his niece. And Pompuss went home, after promising to do all he could for his rich client.

CHAPTER XVII.

"Putting the Screw on."

We again introduce the diligent reader, who has
been sufficiently persevering to get thus far in his
journey through our little book, to Myra.

Very much changed is she from the young lady whom
we last saw kneeling on the *prie-Dieu* in the Highgate
Church.

She is lying on a sofa, dressed in the whitest of spot-
less muslin. The window of the drawing-room is open,
and the sunlight filters into the apartment through the
branches of the trees, which gently wave in the westerly
breeze.

She is pale and attenuated. Her face and hands look
like wax, and her pallor is heightened by the colour of
her dress. Every now and then she sighs deeply, and
her eyes are fixed upon vacancy, and their expression
gone.

Mrs. Pompuss, with the last oracular effusion of the
prophetic Doctor in her hand, sits near her niece.

"The end of all things draweth nigh," she exclaimed.

"I wish I could think so," said Myra.

"Why, are you tired of this life? Do you long for
the Millennium?"

"I long for anything which will rid me of a life
which is irksome beyond the power of endurance."

"Hush, child!" said Mrs. Pompuss, gravely. "Evil
times have come upon us, but it behoves us not to
murmur."

I

A heavy step without announced the arrival from the City of Mr. Pompuss. Hurriedly entering the room, he went up to his niece, and kissed her affectionately on the forehead.

"Well, my little puss," he said, "how are you to-day?"

"I am very ill, uncle," replied Myra. "I cannot disguise from myself the fact that I am gradually sinking."

"What is the cause?"

"Can *you* ask me?" she replied, with an accusing glance.

"I do, in all good faith, my dear. I can see no signs of any hidden malady. None of our family are consumptive. What can it be?"

"A broken heart, I suppose," exclaimed Myra.

An awkward pause ensued.

"Why should your heart be broken?" began Mrs. Pompuss.

"Hold your tongue, 'Liza," said her husband; adding, "I was in hopes that your fancy for Ogilvie, Myra, would pass away as the length of his absence increased. If you really love him so much—that is, if I had known it at the time, I would not have withheld my consent to your union; but, of course, all regret is too late now."

Myra shook her head sadly.

"I met Moskins to-day," continued the stockbroker, addressing himself to no one in particular.

A shudder ran through Myra.

"What did he talk about?" inquired Mrs. Pompuss.

"The price of stocks and shares, and something else."

"Indeed! What was this something else?"

"Our undutiful niece here."

"Undutiful, uncle?" said Myra, raising herself on her elbow. "You cannot call me that; I am anything but undutiful."

" I meant it in reference to my wish—I may say our wish ; for my wife's opinions and my own are identical on that subject. I meant it with reference to my wish that you should marry Mr. Moskins."

" Why should I ?"

" You have for some time been fully aware of several reasons. Let me recapitulate them, and add a few more. I have spent the money left you by your father. It is true that you alone could punish me for that ; but, as it was done as much for your benefit as for my own, you have been good enoughto forgive me. I have been very unlucky lately ; nothing goes right with me. I think the devil's in the business. To-day I sold my house and furniture. Who was the buyer ? Isaac Moskins. He can turn us into the street to-morrow if he likes ; in point of fact, I am completely in that man's power."

" What do you want me to do ?" asked Myra, impatiently.

" My dear ——"

" Will you, please, come to the point ? All this beating about the bush is so intensely fatiguing to me."

" Will you marry Moskins ?" blurted out the stock-broker.

" Will it get you out of your troubles if I do ?" she demanded.

" Yes, it will."

" You are sure ?"

" Perfectly. I should be as right as a trivet in no time."

" That is sufficient. I will be his wife."

" When ?"

" Whenever you like, but ——"

" What ?"

" I warn you," said Myra, " that you had better make haste."

ɪ 2

"Why?" asked Pompuss, puzzled.

"I shall not live long, and you had better get me married soon, unless Mr. Moskins wants a corpse for his bride."

"Myra," said her aunt, warningly, "this levity is most reprehensible."

"It is true, aunt," replied Myra.

Rising in great agitation, Mr. Pompuss exclaimed—

"My dear child, I thank you. Believe me when I say you have saved me from—from—I will not say what."

He left the room.

Myra sighed more deeply than before.

Mrs. Pompuss spoke to her several times without receiving an answer.

"Myra," she exclaimed, "how mad of you! Why do you not — Eh ? What's the matter with the child ?"

Myra had fainted.

CHAPTER XVIII.

" HARD UP."

A SHORT way down a street turning out of the Strand, up three pairs of stairs, resided *pro tem.* Colonel Bowering, his son Billy, and Sir Philip Deverill.

It may be wondered how these worthies made one another's acquaintance, and how they came to be living on the third floor in a third-rate London street.

Everything had failed to prosper with Colonel Bowering. The money he received from Mr. Moskins had been injudiciously invested, and he had lost the bulk of it. Billy Bowering was, of course, dependent upon his father, and shared his fortunes, whatever they might be.

The father and son had made the acquaintance of Sir Philip Deverill on the Stock Exchange. Sir Philip had imprudently allowed himself to be placed on the direction of a bubble company, and be duly qualified. When the company went to the dogs, which it did in its own proper time, Sir Philip was sued as a shareholder, and made a contributory under a winding-up order, which rendered it advisable for him to keep " dark " for a brief space. There was a bedroom to let at 10s. a-week in the house in which Colonel Bowering lodged, and of this Sir Philip took possession.

Bowering did not exactly like the baronet, though he respected him as a man of talent and a sharp practitioner, who, like most very clever men, had got bitten at last.

Sir Philip could not claim to be descended from a long line of ancestors without fear or reproach. His father was no tenth transmitter of a foolish face, but the grandfather had been Lord Mayor during a Royal visit to the City, and the King had made him a baronet. A certain newspaper of the day had been very severe upon him and upon the creation; but there were satirical newspapers in those days as well as in these.

Some of the baronet's enemies having discovered this article in the old paper, very kindly reproduced it on a sheet of note-paper, and handed it about at a board-meeting of the company when it was beginning to fall into disgrace.

It is worth recording here, though we shall not give it *in extenso*.

The journal, which we will call the "Sledge-Hammer," having employed leaded type, said, "We would present our readers with a biographical sketch of the new baronet, if the early years of the Lord Mayor were not wrapped in impenetrable obscurity. Nevertheless, the king has delighted to honour him. Royalty moves in a mysterious way. We must not inquire too closely into its reasons for so doing. Sir Philip Deverill, who, by being made a baronet, is now titled in perpetuity, has, in the words of Malvolio, had greatness thrust upon him. He was not born to greatness, nor can he be said exactly to have taken the tide of fortune at the flood. His accession to rank is rather the result of a happy accident. Such rare birds as kings and princes do not often go east of Temple Bar, and when they are made familiar with civic hospitality, and initiated into the mysteries of the freedom of the City of London, which is usually associated with a casket of curious workman-ship, we suppose it is only fitting and proper that such distinguished services as are rendered by the Lord Mayor for the time being should be substantially re-

warded. Future members of the House of Deverill
will probably be at a loss to discover why they figure
prominently in the pages of Debrett and Lodge, but
they will doubtless find consolation in the old saying,
'*Omne ignotum pro magnifico.*' Badinage apart, we are, in
all candour, compelled to admit that this outpouring of
the vial of Government favour upon the head of the
present chief magistrate of the City of London has not
been so popular in civic circles as would have been supposed. People remember a gentleman who, like the
immortal Whittington, was twice Lord Mayor of London
—who, in spite of his money and great services, was not
rewarded with the substantial recognition his services
deserved. We could mention many other names, but
one instance is quite sufficient to prove the lack of dis-
crimination existing in high places. It is not the
mere pitch-forking of the first prominent individual into
the ranks of our old nobility, if we may so phrase it, that
makes an Administration popular. It is putting the
right man in the right place, and honouring the one to
whom honour is due; and we have great doubts
whether in the present instance this has been done.
From all accounts, Sir Philip Deverill is a man of high
moral character, a Dissenter from the Established
Church, popular amongst the Evangelical party, but
of mediocre ability, which, however, is no bar to dis-
tinction in the opinion of the Prime Minister, who, as
Warwick was called the King-maker, has been favoured
with the distinguishing epithet of ' Bishop-maker,' and
who, for aught we know, may look with peculiar fondness upon the infusion of new blood into the baronetage
of the United Kingdom, and fresh creations generally.
It is admitted, on all hands, that the reception of the
King at the Guildhall was a magnificent affair, excel-
lently well managed. It reflected credit alike upon the
host and upon the illustrious guest in whose honour

the banquet was given. This year will be one memorable in the annals of the City, and perhaps we are wrong, after all, in imagining that the mere fact of receiving the Sovereign and some few of his Ministers is not a sufficient excuse for raising a simple and well-meaning citizen to a pinnacle of the City Temple of Fame, while many of his predecessors infinitely more deserving have been passed over and forced to content themselves with an insignificant niche in the lower regions of the aforesaid edifice. It is good that the loyalty of the citizens should be stimulated occasionally. An architect was lately made a baronet; but it is true we have a fine building to remind us of his skill. Nevertheless, a stimulus will be given to Guildhall banquets, and there will be no stint of turtle and champagne when next the most insignificant sprig of Royalty visits the City. Such prodigality, if it does nothing else, rejoices the hearts of the Common Councilmen and makes it good for trade."

Sir Philip did not care much about this tirade. He had the title, and all he required was a little money to support it in a proper manner.

The triumvirate never allowed a day to pass without plotting and planning something by means of which they could retrieve their shattered fortunes.

Billy Bowering generally sat still and listened, or lounged on the sofa, smoking, and drinking bottled beer. They had three bed-rooms and a sitting-room, which was the whole of the third floor; and being at the top of the house, they did pretty much as they liked, cooking for themselves occasionally, with the help of a small boy whom they called indifferently, owing to his being one of Pharaoh's lean kine, and his diminutive size generally, " Shadow " and the " Aztec."

Though called a boy, this atomic specimen of the

genus homo or more correctly *homun-culus,* was at least sixteen, and as sharp and clever as one twice his age.

It was a very wet day. The rain had commenced falling at eight in the morning, and continued to descend with a steady, pitiless malice prepense, which made walking a misery. Down it came in a merciless shower, making every gutter a small rivulet, and washing the face of the big city. The triumvirate were confined to the house. Sir Philip wanted to go down to the City, which he ventured to do occasionally, but Colonel Bowering over-ruled him, saying—

"You know there will be little or no business doing. Prices usually rule low on wet days, and the markets are flat. Besides, you are not quite safe. A tap on the shoulder might convey you to that vile region where the impecunious most do congregate. Stop at home, and chat. We may hit upon something to get us out of the hobble we are in ; and if the time hangs heavy on our hands, why, we can have a game at loo."

"For what ?" asked Sir Philip. "Sugar plums or haricot beans ?"

"Oh, hang it all !" exclaimed Billy Bowering ; "we are not so bad as that yet. I have a few pounds ; though how long they will last I won't be so rash as to predict."

"You have the advantage of me," said Sir Philip ; "for I have only the change out of a sovereign ; though an option I did last week will bring me in something at the fortnightly account ; at least, it looks healthy enough at present. Is there any beer in that bottle ?"

"None," said Billy, taking it up and giving it a shake. "It's as empty as—as—give me a simile, some of you."

"Your head, Billy," suggested his father.

"That's too bad of you," said Billy, "seeing that I inherited the *caput* from you, and you are responsible for its manufacture. Never mind ; send the Aztec to the pub. for another half-dozen."

"Reckless extravagance ! Never mind ; I'll toss you who pays for it. Sudden death ! a man ! It is, by Jove ! Billy, you re in for it."

Billy put his hand in his pocket, took out half-a-sovereign, and began to make a most unearthly noise, which had the effect of producing the Aztec from an adjoining apartment.

"Here, Shadow," he said, "you saw me order half-a-dozen of Bass yesterday, and pay for them. Well, go and do likewise."

The boy took the money, and was going off, when his master cried—

"Bow, you beggar! You're forgetting all the amenities of civilization, and becoming a perfect savage. I shall have to stop your growth. Be off."

When the Shadow had vanished, Sir Philip said—

"I like to toss with Billy. He parts so gracefully ; doesn't he ?"

"Takes it like a lamb, Sir," answered the Colonel.

"That sufficiently proves the nature of my parentage," observed Billy, complacently.

There was a laugh. The Shadow returned with the beer, and, lighting cigars, the trio ruminated. Suddenly Colonel Bowering said—

"I wish to God I knew how I could be revenged on that paper-faced, white-livered fellow, Moskins."

"Easily enough, my boy," said Sir Philip.

"How's that ?"

"Go and Bear the shares of the Agha and Plasterman's ; get up a panic ; speculate yourself in the shares for the fall. The bank shuts up, you make your own fortune, and ruin your enemy."

"Ah!" exclaimed Colonel Bowering; "that idea has occured to me ; but the difficulty of the thing has always prevented me from putting it into execution."

"A few anonymous letters would be the thing," put in Billy.

"I hate the very name and suspicion of anything anonymous," said the Colonel.

"Degenerate boy!" said Sir Philip Deverill, with a smile.

"That's all rot," replied Billy. "When fellows are as down on their luck and as hard up as we are, it is not to be supposed that they will stick at anything to put themselves in coin. I see visions of bullion in the future. Let us get a list of the shareholders of the Agha Bank, and write a lot of letters calculated to funk them. I think we have got a little credit with our brokers. Let us sell at the same time, and the shares are bound. to drop, because one out of every twenty letters will hit a nervous old fellow who won't stay to inquire into the truth of our insinuations, but draw out at once."

The Aztec lad put his head in at the door.

"What is it, Aztec?" asked Sir Philip.

"Paper's come, Sir."

"Send it back, then. If it can't come before twelve, it may stop at Printing-house-square, for all I care."

"No ; bring it here. I want to have a look at it," said Colonel Bowering, taking it from the lad's hand.

He turned the pages over, running his eye rapidly, in a practised manner, up and down the columns.

"Hey!" he exclaimed.

"What's the matter? Any one we know gone dead?" asked Billy.

"Something has occurred which will materially assist us in our plans." answered the Colonel.

"Bravo! The luck's changing. I knew it would," cried Billy.

"What is it?" asked Sir Philip, anxiously.

"Only the Metropolitan Union."

"Gone ?"

"Yesterday afternoon."

"By George! there will be a run on all the banks now," said Sir Philip. "I can see the course events will take as clearly as possible. I'll run into the City and bring back some intelligence. You and Billy can write some of the letters while I'm gone."

"I shall be going out, too, later in the day. Billy and I will meet you at the ' Widow's.' "

"Very well," answered Sir Philip, putting on his hat. "I know where I can borrow a hundred. I'll do it, and Bear Agha shares on spec."

So saying, he threw his cigar away, took up an umbrella, and started for the City.

"Can you write a letter, dad ?" asked Billy.

"I don't know. I'm not great at literary composition, but I daresay we can knock up the sort of thing between us."

"We'll make a feeble effort."

"You write, then, and I'll make a start. 'Sir.' Got that ?"

"Yes," said Billy. "There isn't much difficulty about that. I could have got as far as that myself."

"'Sir,—Although I do not, for obvious reasons, choose to allow my name to appear in this letter, yet I am personally known to you, and wish you well.' Got that ?"

Billy nodded.

"'I consider it my imperative duty to—to—' Got that ?"

"Imperative duty. Yes."

"To—to—. You take a spell, now, Billy. The Muse isn't kind. I've worked the vein out."

"All right," said Billy, who began writing away rapidly. When he stopped, he said—

"Shall I read it ?"

" Fire away !" said his father.

" ' I consider it my imperative duty to warn you that the Agha Bank is in difficulties, which must eventually render it bankrupt. The state of affairs in India is such that the bank cannot last many weeks if the present frightful panic in the City continues. You, Sir, have worked hard to earn a competence to maintain yourself and family. It would grieve me much to see you brought to the workhouse by no fault of your own ; therefore I say emphatically, ask no questions, but at once withdraw your account. This is no idle letter. Follow the advice it contains, and all will be well ; neglect it, and ruin stares you in the face.' "

" Capital ! Billy, you're a genius !" exclaimed Colonel Bowering.

" Will it do ?" inquired the author, caressing his moustache.

" Famously."

" ' Ruin stares you in the face.' That's neat, I flatter myself. 'See you brought to the workhouse ' ain't bad, either. It touches them up, you know. Fancy an old Indian with three thousand a-year contemplating such a contingency."

" That will do, Billy, my boy. You and I will sit up with Deverill to-night, and knock off a couple of hundred. We'll send the Agha to smash, and ruin Moskins yet."

With this charitable prediction on his lips, he opened a fresh bottle of beer, and refreshed the inner man. Not that the inner man stood in need of refreshing, but it was a way he had. Drinking at irregular intervals was a necessity with him.

CHAPTER XIX.

The Anonymous Letter.

If the polish of Hazlitt could be mingled with the lively humour of Goldsmith—if the terseness of Bacon could be added to the vivacity and truthfulness to nature of Steele and Addison, and be concentrated in one gifted individual,—we should probably possess a perfect essayist, but as such a combination is scarcely likely to take place, the gentle readers of the present generation must be content to

"Take the goods the gods provide them,"

and be thankful for small mercies when great are conspicuous by their absence.

If we possessed the requisite pen-power, we should be tempted to write an essay upon the " Widow's," as the tavern at which the triumvirate agreed to meet was called; and yet not so much upon the house itself as upon those who frequented it, and whose lights have too long been hidden under impenetrable bushels.

It was late in the day when the Bowerings, *père et fils*, arrived. The bar was full. Sir Philip brought intelligence of the failure of another bank, and the draft of the anonymous letter was shown him.

"So far, so good," he said. "Let us leave business till the evening. Now is the time to smoke the pipe of peace, and drink the something glass."

"Cheering," suggested Billy.

"That will do. Order three brandies. Do you

know any of the fellows here? No? I used to be on tolerably good terms with them all. They are chiefly literary men. Look at that gentleman with a grey coat, a well-brushed hat, and scrupulously clean boots. He has a slight stoop in the shoulders, as if accustomed to bend over a desk; his eyes, having no celestial tendency, seek the ground like those of ruminating quadrupeds. He has just completed an article for the *Daily Banner*, a paper which considers itself a power in the State, and he is thinking what he shall say about Reform and Beales, M.A., and his congenial Odgerses and Potters, for a leader in next week's *Saturday Slasher*. He likes this old-fashioned tavern, which has evidently gone through dirt to dignity, if one may judge from its dingy exterior. It is a house of call for authors who feel that the fire of genius is in danger of expiring unless it is sustained by the dew off Ben Nevis or *Vieux Cognac*. In strict justice, however, I am bound to admit that there are other inducements for visiting the 'Widow's' than that of dram-drinking. The facile contributor to the *Daily Banner* will probably meet that clever and well-known serial writer whose fertile brain has long enriched and adorned the columns of the *Domestic's Delight*. Near him, rapidly succumbing to the influence of repeated 'cold gins,' is another well-known gentleman, whose tales, written under the *nom de plume* of Lord Claude Forteskewer in the pages of the *Halfpenny Tempter*, delighted the town, and gave the million such a veracious insight into the manners and customs of the Upper Ten. That man is another journalist. Do you see how cordially welcomed he is? That little man, of light complexion, whose voice has a sound like that of a Japanese guitar when strummed on by native fingers, is a sort of hanger-on of the other men."

Billy Bowering listened attentively, and watched the

little man, who approached the journalist and asked
him if he would stand anything. The great man refused, on the ground of impecuniosity, and the little
man found that he had unnecessarily humiliated himself. He turned pale, as visions of long ago borrowed,
but still unpaid, sixpences rose before him. He recognized the mournful fact that he had gone to the end of
his tether, and that no more eleemosynary grogs would
be bestowed upon him by the great writer of leaders.

"Who is that fellow?" asked Billy, pointing to a
short, dapper little man.

"Oh! I see. I'll tell you. I'll tell you who they
all are," answered Sir Philip. "The man you mean is
the versatile editor of the *Penny Pieman*, a periodical
circulating chiefly amongst the lower orders of society.
This paper has lately amalgamated with the *Great Un-
washed*, and is now advocating an extension of the
franchise, which it claims as a democratic right, and
not, as Mr. Disraeli calls it, a popular privilege. The
editor prides himself upon his answers to correspondents ;
the fact being that the replies are generally inaccurate
and always ungrammatical. To the right I detect the
genial countenance of Mr. Limner, the artist, who has
spoilt more wood than a moderate-sized house would
take to build. His pictorial women are always alike,
and, people say, are faithful portraits of his wife as she
appeared in those days when Mr. L. led her to the altar.
His *forte* is the delineation of human beings in a state
of dissolution brought about by physical violence. His
incised wounds are admitted by the faculty to be exact
anatomical studies, and he can sever the carotid artery
with the grace of an accomplished cut-throat. Engaged
in earnest conversation with Mr. Limner is another
artist, who has devoted the whole of his undeniable
talent to the well-developed figures of ballet girls and
actresses. His Menken was thought a work of art. His

Eve in the Biche-au-bois is still spoken of, but his fame rests on Cora Pearl as Cupidon at the Bouffes, and a grand character group representing Mr. Gus. Harris's incomparable *Forty Thieves* at Covent Garden. That man who drinks with everybody and never puts down his glass until it is empty is the talented author of the ' Frantic Princesses of London ; or, the Wild Mohawks of the Starless Night,' which appeared in penny numbers, and has not yet arrived at the dignity of being bound. Miss Braddon says somewhere that the penny public like their literature as they like their pudding, in penny slices. The gentleman whom I am describing is the great high priest of this section of the community. I may say that occasionally literary talent does not care for trifles—such as dress, for instance. Observe the author of the ' Frantic Princesses ': his coat is profusely ornamented with that delicate substance, of doubtful origin and obscure end, that men call fluff. The use of a brush is discarded as a vanity, and a clean collar is clearly a pomp. The nap of his hat is restless. The Yankees speak of whiskey in the hair; does it, I wonder, ever get into one's hat ? He is now engaged on the ' Fearful Phantoms of the Isle of Dogs ; or, the Dark Demons of the Dismal Ditches.' He is fond of alliteration, as will have been perceived, and is thinking of suggesting to an enterprising publisher ' The Weird Wanderers of Wenham Lake and the Ice Islands of the Inland Sea.' His greatest success was the ' Red Cripple,' published some years back in ' The Unwelcome Intruder,' with which was incorporated the ' Weekly Visitor.' Leaving him, I come to an individual of a very wild, not to say formidable, aspect. He is commonly reported to have long resided amongst the Polynesians, and to have been intimately acquainted with those experimentalists in gastronomy, yclept cannibals. His hair is unkempt, and his mode of locomotion is that of a gouty bear. His fame rests principally upon tales of travels, such as 'Below the Surface; or, a Voyage inside a Shark from Labrador to San Francisco,' with a few words on Jonah. His 'Lost among the Wahabees and found on the top of Snowdon' was also a great success; while Messrs. Pottiton and Pegaway, his publishers, are said to have sold five thousand copies of his 'Invisible Kraken' in less than a month. That tall man who affects a Dundreary manner has a three years' engagement on the 'Sere and Yellow Leaf,' an old maids' journal. He is writing an affecting tale of the Richardson kind, and he visits the Museum to read 'Pamela.' Near him is a man who is chiefly remarkable for being related to some men who are admitted to be writers of talent."

The busy bees in this hive do not stop very long at the "Widow's." They leave the drones to hang about the bar and smoke short pipes, until they come back again, for it is a sacred duty to have a final "drain" at the "Widow's" before they separate and pass out into the growing darkness, made visible by the sickly glare of the street lamps.

Billy laughed immoderately at the humorous description which Sir Philip Deverill had given of his *quondam* acquaintances at the tavern.

That night saw the three men very busy. When Colonel Bowering saw his way to making a good thing, you may be sure he did not suffer the grass to grow under his feet. They wrote between them nearly a hundred letters, and at five o'clock in the morning, when the grey dawn was being streaked with red, Billy Bowering went out with a little bag on his arm, and posted them in batches of five and ten at different post-offices.

So they shot their shaft, and hoped for good results.

CHAPTER XX.

" SHALL I DO THIS THING ?"

ALTHOUGH Myra Fontaine had solemnly pledged her word to Mr. Pompuss that she would marry Mr. Isaac Moskins, she was far from feeling happy or contented now that she had arrived at this decision.

She knew that she was making an immense sacrifice of inclination at the shrine of duty; but that comforted her slightly. Frank Ogilvie, she felt certain, would live and die single, for her sake. Oh! how she longed sometimes to sell all her jewellery and fine dresses to raise a sum of money with which she could fly to that distant and savage land where Frank was expending his energies, and pining for the love she withheld! If she were to say to him, "Frank, I recall my determination,"—if she were even to write this to him, she knew that, as soon as it was possible, he would be kneeling at her feet.

Mr. Moskins had to go to Vienna on business; so the marriage was put off for a month until his return, when it was to be solemnized with the greatest pomp at St. George's, Hanover-square.

No criminal condemned to death ever received a reprieve on the morning of the day appointed for his execution with greater joy than did Myra accept this welcome intelligence.

Not a line had she received from Frank since his departure; but he, nevertheless, had contrived to communicate with her, for he had written to a mutual friend, speaking of the work before him in the most

K 2

glowing terms, uttering a few kindly words about Myra, which he knew would be repeated to her. And yet he flattered himself that he had behaved like a stoic, forgetting the past, and thrown himself, heart and soul into his mission, forgetting that "*Qui fecit per alium fecit perse.*"

Myra felt that every hour she passed as Isaac Moskins' wife would be equivalent to imbibing an infinitesimal quantity of a subtle poison, none the less virulent because it was imperceptible, because the atoms would gradually amount to sufficient to destroy her life. She was sacrificing herself for the sake of the bad, weak man whom her father had placed in the stead of a parent to her. It was to keep him and his wife from the workhouse that she was doing this.

All at once the chief instigator, Mr. Pompuss, fell grievously sick. Over-work and worry had brought on a complete prostration of the system, and the doctors— some of them—said he could not recover. With many tears, Mrs. Pompuss recognized the fact, and with that passivity which her religion encouraged, she bowed her head to the storm.

"Myra, my dear," she said, drawing her to her one evening, when Pompuss had fallen asleep upstairs, and they could get down into the fresher air of the sitting-room, "Myra, I am very much afraid that my poor husband is not long for this world. The hand of the Lord has been heavy upon us of late. For myself I don't much care, yet I could have wished it otherwise."

"We must hope for the best, dear aunt," said Myra, taking her hand and pressing it tenderly, as if to assure her of her sympathy.

"I have hoped against hope until all hope is gone," answered the poor woman. "I had hoped that your marriage with Mr. Moskins would have placed us in a better position."

" And will it not ?"

" I trust not. And I will tell you why. The match was one chiefly of my husband's making. Poor fellow ! he had set his heart upon it, and I, falling in with his inclination, did my best to make you consent ; but now, with the fear of death before his eyes, I don't think he would want you to make the sacrifice, because it would do him no good. Those who die by the way cannot enjoy the sweets which are to be met with at the journey's end."

" But yourself ? You have forgotten yourself, dear aunt," exclaimed Myra.

" Oh, no. I would rather pass the remainder of my days in a workhouse than you should make a match distasteful and odious to you, to keep me surrounded with those luxuries I have for many years enjoyed. But you need be under no apprehension about me. I have already made an application to a House of Charity, as it is called, and the authorities have agreed to accept me as an inmate. Be not shocked, my child. It is an excellent institution, founded by some kind and charitable person, for the relief of decayed gentlewomen, and secures them a quiet old age and a *euthanasia*."

Myra's eyes burned brightly, but she said nothing.

" What I would advise is this," continued Mrs. Pompuss. " Seek your uncle ; tell him the decision I have come to, and ask him boldly, 'Shall I do this thing?' If he releases you from your promise, and it pleases the Lord to take him, I daresay we shall be able to raise money enough for you to go to the country where Frank Ogilvie has gone, and where your heart is."

" You are kind—generous ; you overwhelm me. I must think of this," cried Myra, speaking thickly.

" Take your time, my dear. I have not done too much good in my time that I should neglect this opportunity of making two people happy."

Late in the evening, Myra heard her uncle's bell
ring, and she went upstairs, receiving an encouraging
smile from her aunt.   Mr. Pompuss was lying, much ex-
hausted, upon his bed.   The pomposity of manner which
had characterized him in the early days of his introduc-
tion to the reader had entirely disappeared; he was
meek and humble enough now.   Suffering and severe
bodily illness had done their work.   He had gone
through the fire, and been purified.   Going to the bed-
side, Myra arranged the clothes and placed his pillows in
a more comfortable shape for him.

He thanked her in a low voice, and when she asked
him if he were any better, he replied in the negative.

"I'm afraid I'm booked, Myra," he said.   "My lease
has run out.   We all owe Heaven a debt, and I shall
pay my debt a little before the time."

"I hope not, uncle.   You are low-spirited, and do not
take a cheerful view of things."

"You are very good to try and cheer me up; but I
can't shut my eyes to facts," he said, shaking his head
in a melancholy manner.

"If you were strong enough, I wanted to speak to
you," she said, timidly, casting down her eyes.

"Well enough?   Why, yes, I am well enough," he
answered.   "You are talking to me now.   What is it—
eh?"

"Nothing much, uncle.   Perhaps I had better post-
pone it," said Myra, blundering dreadfully.

Her eyes wandered round the room, counting the
chairs, the medicine-bottles on the mantelpiece, looking
at the open Bible on a table,—seeking anything, in fact,
but the eyes of the sick man.

"I am quite as strong now as I shall be, I fear," he
exclaimed; "so you need not scruple to tell me anything which you have on your mind."

She still hesitated, and he proceeded to make an obser-
vation which rendered her task yet more difficult.

" It is hard for me to be thus ill," he exclaimed ; " because I had looked forward to your marriage with
Moskins. Yet I have one consolation, and that is, your
union with the rich man will make your poor aunt
happy. It will be a comfort to me to know that she is
provided for. You know how fastidious she is, poor
thing, Myra ; and she would feel the deprivation of all
her little luxuries—wouldn't she ?"

Myra made some reply—she scarcely knew what—and
was more directly recalled to herself by her uncle, who
said—

" And, now, my child, if you will forgive me for the interruption, I shall be glad to hear what you have to
say."

" It was about—about this marriage, uncle," she
gasped.

" With Moskins ?" asked the invalid, turning a shade
paler, if possible.

" Yes."

" What about it ?"

" Why, only this. Aunt said—that is, if you are so ill
that you cannot live to enjoy the result of—of my
marriage with Mr. Moskins, aunt—she said ——"

Here she broke down entirely.

Mr. Pompuss regarded her suspiciously.

" Go on," he said, sternly.

" She said—that is, aunt said she would not care
about me making the sac—sacrifice for her only, and—
and it is a dreadful thing to say to you, because it turns
upon your life or death ; but I must say it," she continued, as if talking to herself, and wringing her hands
in agony, " I must say it. You have heard me, and, I
hope, understood me ; and all I have to add is, shall I
do this thing ?"

And John Pompuss answered—

" Yes."

CHAPTER XXI.

DECKING THE VICTIM.

THE stern, hard voice in which her uncle spoke convinced Myra that it would be useless to ask him again to release her from her promise. How she got away from the room she did not know ; but she remembered, the next morning, seeking her aunt, telling her, in a few words, how her hopes were dashed, and weeping with bitter tears as she rested her head on her bosom.

The news from the City became worse every day, and, though not now in business, Mr. Pompuss took the greatest interest in the City Article in the daily papers. So did Mr. Moskins. Telegrams reached him in Vienna, telling him of the deplorable state of the Money Market. Scarcely a day passed without a bank breaking. Things went from bad to worse. People went about with 'bated breath, wondering which bank would go next, and who was to be ruined first. Speculation was a dead letter. Enterprise was knocked on the head. The Bears had it all their own way. The great discount houses toppled over, and they in their turn dragged down the mammoth railway contractors.

In the midst of the almost universal crash, the Agha and Plasterman's stood its ground, but the run upon it was unprecedented in banking annals. Isaac Moskins heard the sinister rumours which were afloat, and came back to London in a state of abject terror. He had made millions, but it seemed there was a chance of his losing them again. Now he blamed his supine folly at not withdrawing his account when he first heard whispers as to the critical state of the bank's finances. He had been "too sharp by half." In the first rush of the storm he should have withdrawn his account, though he might have caused the failure of the bank. That fact, however, would have troubled him little, so long as he could have preserved his fortune, which he doubted his ability to do now. Nervously he sought the manager of the bank, and found him in close confabulation with the directors. He asked if he could have his money, and they told him frankly, "No. He could not have a tenth part of it. Their only chance of weathering the storm was to go on paying the small accounts, and restore the confidence of the public. If they could only achieve this, all would be well, and in the course of time Mr. Moskins might have his money." In the meantime he was implored not to withdraw anything, but to wait. So he waited. Very ill at ease was he, but it was Hobson's choice, and he could not help himself.

As Mr. Pompuss continued so ill, Mr. Moskins began to fear he would die, and that event would put off his marriage with Myra for at least six months. So he got him removed to Buxton, to try the waters there; and, strange to say, the change did him good; and in a fortnight he was so much better, that it was deemed advisable to proceed with the marriage, which it was arranged should be solemnized at Buxton, and not at Hanover-square, as previously spoken of. Although Moskins had been told that Pompuss was ill, he was far from imagining how ill he really was. He found the family in a large house in a large, open street. The stockbroker held out a hot, burning, feverish hand to him, and hoped he was well, with his usual half-fawning, partly abject manner. He was always more or less abject when speaking to this possessor of millions, because he had had it in his power to do him so much harm and so much good.

"A little better are you?" said Moskins. "That's right. How's the wife and niece?"

"The wife's well enough, thank you; and so is Myra. They have gone for a walk, but will be in shortly. I expected them before now. They are late."

"I've brought a beautiful set of diamonds for Myra, and must put them on the dear girl when she returns."

"So generous," said Pompuss, rubbing his hands. "But it's like you. You always were the most open-handed fellow I ever met with; always said so to people—did, indeed. How were the banks when you left? Shaky, I suppose?"

"Everything's shaky, Sir. The funds have dropped two per cent. since this time yesterday. The Central and Suburban Discount's gone. Did you hear that?"

"No. Bless me! The Central and Suburban? Who'd have thought it? Many a bill of mine have they had, Sir—many and many a bill. My paper was good there to the tune of thirty thousand once. That was the accommodation they gave me; and I'd nearly as much in half-a-dozen other places. Those were the days!"

"The Agha will get over it," remarked Moskins.

"It will—eh? Glad to hear it. A good bank, Sir; always thought well of it. So it will pull through? I suppose you are not much concerned there? Wise in time—eh?"

"Trust me," answered the millionaire, with a knowing look.

Presently Myra came in with her aunt, looking tired, but wearing a healthy colour, imparted to her cheeks by the fresh country air and exercise.

Seizing her by the hand, Mr. Moskins kissed her, saying—

"I am tempted to steal one kiss. You must forgive me. I have my way before marriage; you have yours afterwards. Is not that the ordinary arrangement?"

Myra shuddered, but did not evince the least resentment. Whatever her thoughts were, she carefully concealed them.

"Why, Mr. Moskins," exclaimed Mrs. Pompuss, "I declare, you're getting quite thin! Those German baths, or something or other, have been too much for your system. You will require a little of my nursing to set you right again."

"That's well said. We'll nurse him. Oh, yes; we'll nurse him," said the stockbroker, in a tremulous voice, which he intended to be full of hilarity, but which he could not steady in the least, and which bore about as much resemblance to mirth as does the croak of a raven.

"I've got a little surprise for Myra," exclaimed Moskins; "a little present, in fact, if she will honour me by accepting such a trifle."

Opening a carpet-bag, he displayed some morocco leather cases. Snapping a spring, the largest one flew open. It contained a mass of diamonds, which sparkled so brilliantly that it positively made Mrs. Pompuss blink to look at it. All the boxes were opened one after the other, and the good lady's exclamations of delight were loud and frequent.

"Well, I never did!" she said. "It's a present fit for a Queen. It is, really. Myra, why don't you thank the gentleman, as he deserves?"

"I'm very grateful, aunt; I am, indeed," said Myra.

"Don't want any gratitude," remarked Mr. Moskins. "So long as you're pleased, I'm sure I'm satisfied. Let me try them on; do, please."

"Yes, do, Myra," exclaimed Mrs. Pompuss, eagerly.

"Come and put on a low dress. It's nearly dinner-time."

Seizing her hand, she dragged her out of the room. Myra followed her up the stairs to the bed-room, without saying a word; but when she got there, she burst into tears, and cried as if her heart was going to break.

"Why, bless me! what's the matter now? Well, you are the most curious girl. Don't you see your uncle is getting better, and that your marriage will make him well again. The prospect of regaining his health and being set up in business again, is doing him more good than all the air and the doctors."

"Oh, aunt!" sobbed Myra, "you didn't talk like this a month ago."

"I did not, because I thought all hope was gone, and I felt chastened. But you cannot question my love for my husband; and when I see him coming to his health again, I—I— You know what I mean, Myra. I cannot find it in my heart, my dear, to say one word which will induce you to break your word, and—and I hope you will be happy—very happy with Mr. Moskins, as his wife, for very many years."

"Thank you, aunt. I believe you mean well," said Myra. "But I sha'n't live many years; I sha'n't survive it long."

"Survive it! What nonsense you talk. Don't you know that we ought all of us to be resigned to what is the will of the Lord?" said the good lady, waxing a little indignant as she became piously inclined.

"I don't believe that this marriage is the will of the Lord. But it has to take place, and it is no use repining; though I am not a log of wood, and have more feeling than those about me give me credit for."

"That is sensible, my dear child," replied her aunt, soothingly. "It is all for the best, believe me. Your friends are older, and must know better than you. What we do we do for your good."

So wrapt up was she in the belief in her own benevolence, that she actually believed what she was saying. So true it is that we may in the course of time, by a particular process of reasoning, deceive ourselves.

"Besides, my dear," she went on, " poverty is such a dreadful thing. We began to experience its bitterness; and I, for one, shrank from it. It is true I wrote to the House of Charity, but that was when hope was dead within me, and I thought I had nothing left to live for. But now that John is coming round again, I feel that I can enjoy life with the best of them."

This speech made Myra think there was more selfishness in human nature than she had imagined. Drying her tears, she began to change her dress.

Mrs. Pompuss continued her lecture, and, unhappily, touched a chord which jarred painfully.

"If it was not for the money, I would, as you know, rather see you the wife of Frank than of any one, because Frank —— "

"Please—*please*, don't, dear aunt," said Myra, beseechingly. " I can't bear to hear *his* name. If you wish me to bear up at all, try to keep his image away from me."

"I beg your pardon, I'm sure. I didn't mean any harm, as you know. It was mere thoughtlessness."

In time Myra was dressed, and Mrs. Pompuss assured her that she had never looked better.

"A low dress is generally becoming to young people," she said ; " but you look positively ravishing in one. Those diamonds are worthily bestowed. What beauties! They must have cost a very large sum. Well, I don't know whether I would not rather be an old man's darling, when the old man is rich, than a young man's slave. What, tears again ! What have I said? How sensitive you are ! There, wipe your cheeks, and put a little powder on. Dry your eyes. That is better."

The cloth, of snowy whiteness, was laid for dinner. The wine stood in coolers on the sideboard. Beautiful flowers raised their lovely heads in a magnificent epergne. Mr. Pompuss and the millionaire were standing by the fire-place, talking in a friendly way.

"Ah! here you are, Miss Myra," said Moskins. "Now, let me adorn you."

The victim stepped up to his side, and stood still while he decked her with gems.

"There!" he cried, when the snap of the last clasp informed her that all the ornaments were on; "no princess in London could look better."

"They are very beautiful," observed Myra.

"They do not represent a tenth part of what shall be yours, dearest," said Mr. Moskins, in a low tone.

A servant entering with the soup, Myra was handed to a chair, and the dinner commenced.

CHAPTER XXII.

A Marvellous Telegram.

The day—the fatal day—came. The wedding dress was ordered, and Myra was ready to give her hand, but not her heart, to Isaac Moskins.

During the night Myra had a curious dream. She dreamt that she was walking, in her sleep, dangerously near a precipice, when Frank Ogilvie dropped, as it were, from the clouds, and rescued her from her perilous position.

Mr. Pompuss did not feel well enough on the marriage-day to accompany the party to church; so he remained behind, thinking over the golden future, and congratulating himself upon speedy restoration to health, and another start in business.

The party had not been gone ten minutes before there was a ring of the bell, and a loud knock at the door. Shortly afterwards a servant entered with a piece of paper on a silver salver.

"What is it? Something about the wedding cake, I suppose? Leave it till Mrs. Pompuss comes home. I really have not strength to be worried with these matters of detail."

"It's a telegram, Sir," said the domestic.

"A telegram, is it? For me? Are you sure it is for me?" asked the stockbroker, adjusting his spectacles with trembling fingers.

"Yes, Sir. Here's your name. Will you sign the paper, as the boy's waiting?"

Mr. Pompuss did so, and then took up the telegram, and read it. It was from Frank Ogilvie, and ran as follows :—

"Just returned to London. A relation has left me by will upwards of £100,000. I hear Myra is on the eve of marriage with Mr. Moskins. Apprise her of my return, and save her life and my own by an act of justice. I hear in the City that the Agha and Plasterman's Bank has just suspended payment."

"Here! hi!" cried Mr. Pompuss, ringing the bell violently. "Give me my hat. Call a fly. Make haste, for the love of God, or I shall be too late, and my niece will marry a pauper! Run for a fly!"

Finding his hat, he reached the hall-door just as a fly came up. Getting in, he ordered the man to drive him at the top of his speed to the church, where he arrived at a critical moment.

The ceremony was progressing, and a few more minutes would have seen Myra irretrievably joined in holy wedlock to a man she detested beyond all created beings.

Dashing into the church with his hat on, to the horror of the beadle, Mr. Pompuss waved the telegram above his head, and giving every one the impression that he was raving mad, exclaimed—

"Frank Ogilvie's come home, worth £100,000. The Agha Bank's gone, and you sha'n't marry a man you don't like."

Isaac Moskins' face assumed a ghastly pallor. The book fell from his hands, and he grasped the Communion rails for support.

"You are mad!" he gasped, speaking with difficulty. "The Agha has not gone. It's a lie. It—it couldn't go."

"Is this true, uncle?" asked Myra, addressing Mr. Pompuss.

"Read for yourself, my pet," he replied, handing her the telegram.

When she had satisfied herself, she said—

"Mr. Moskins, you may form what opinion you like of me, but I cannot now marry you."

"A curse upon it! This is the second time the cup has been dashed from my lips."

" I am sorry ——"

"You are not. Why stoop to a conventional falsehood?"

"This scene," exclaimed the officiating clergyman, "is becoming a scandal. If, as I presume, the service is not to be concluded, will you do me the favour to adjourn to the vestry?"

Myra, her aunt, and uncle, were moving away in obedience to this request, when Moskins seized her arm, saying—

"You'll give me the diamonds. I'll start again with the diamonds."

She assured him he was perfectly welcome to every present he had given her, and walked away radiant as the morn, almost delirious with a joy she had never dared to hope for.

    *   *   *   *

It was all true.

Colonel Bowering and his confederates had wrought the ruin of the Agha Bank, and Isaac Moskins found he had been "too sharp by half," for he was at the bottom of the ladder again, after tasting the joys which the possession of fabulous wealth would give to such a man.

Frank Ogilvie had received news of the death of a rich relation from whom he had always had expectations, but who would do nothing for him during his lifetime. He was, by this event, the owner of a hundred thousand pounds, and met with no resistance from any one when he once more offered himself to Myra.

When united, they experienced such happiness as only those who have suffered deeply can enjoy; though their felicity was a little marred by the death of Mr. Pompuss, whose malady was too deeply seated to admit of a cure.

Frank obtained a living in a most picturesque part of England, leaving the aborigines, who had formerly absorbed his attention, to the care of some other enterprising spirit; and so altered is Myra's disposition that he calls her the sunbeam in his house, for she has forgotten sorrow, and her heart is a temple of joy.

THE END.

PRINTED BY WILLIAM JOHN JOHNSON, 121, FLEET STREET, LONDON, E.C

STANDARD AUTHORS.
ONE SHILLING.
Fcap. 8vo, with Illustrated Covers, and well printed on good paper.

When ordering, the Numbers only need be given.

VOL.

1 Confidences
By Author of " Carr of Carrlyon."

2 Erlesmere; or, Contrasts of Character. *By L. S. Lavenu.*

3 Nanette and Her Lovers
By Talbot Gwynne.

4 Life and Death of Silas Barnstarke. *By Talbot Gwynne.*

6 Tender and True
By Author of "Clara Morison."

7 Gilbert Massenger
By Holme Lee.

8 Thorney Hall *By Holme Lee.*

10 The Cruelest Wrong of All
By Author of " Margaret."

12 Hawksview *By Holme Lee.*

14 Florence Templar
By Mrs. F. Vidal.

16 Wheat and Tares : a Modern Story

17 Guilty Peace; or, Amberhill
By A. I. Barrowcliffe.

24 Moulded Out of Faults; or, Adrian L'Estrange

27 Skirmishing
By Author of " Cousin Stella."

28 Farina; a Legend of Cologne
By George Meredith.

29 Normanton *Author of "Amberhill."*

31 The School for Fathers
By Talbot Gwynne.

32 Lena; or, the Silent Woman
By Author of " Beyminstre."

34 Entanglements
By Author of " Mr. Arle," " Caste," &c.

36 Counterparts; or, the Cross of Love *Author of " My First Season."*

38 Extremes *By E. Welliher Atkinson.*

VOL.

40 Uncle Crotty's Relations
By Herbert Glyn.

42 A Bad Beginning *Mrs. Macquoid.*

43 Heiress of the Blackburnfoot
By Author of " A Life's Love."

50 £200 Reward.
Author of " Married Beneath Him."

51 Aunt Margaret's Trouble
By Author of " Mabel's Progress."

52 On the Line and Danger Signal *By Bracebridge Hemyng.*

55 Belial *By a Popular Writer.*

59 Blithedale Romance
By N. Hawthorne.

60 Lovers of Ballyvookan
By Capt. Esmonde White.

62 Paul Gosslett's Confessions
By Charles Lever.

63 Humorous Stories
Author of " Married Beneath Him."

64 Our Widow.
Author of " Married Beneath Him."

65 Tragedy of Life.
By John H. Brenten.

66 A Marine Residence.
By Author of " Our Widow."

67 Tuggs's at Ramsgate.
By Charles Dickens.

68 Rival Houses.
By G. P. R. James.

69 The Man with "the Plums."
By Douglas Jerrold.

70 Killed by Mistake.
By Edward Mayhew.

71 Box for the Season.
C. C. Clarke.

72 Mr. Ledbury. *Albert Smith.*

73 An Ocean Waif. *G. M. Fenn.*

London: CHAPMAN & HALL, 193, Piccadilly.